COOL PURSUIT

CHAOS CORE BOOK 2

RANDOLPH LALONDE

BOOKS BY RANDOLPH LALONDE

THE CHAOS CORE SERIES

Trapped

Cool Pursuit

Savage Stars

THE SPINWARD FRINGE SERIES

Spinward Fringe Broadcast 0: Origins

Spinward Fringe Broadcast 1 and 2: Resurrection and Awakening

Spinward Fringe Broadcast 3: Triton

Spinward Fringe Broadcast 4: Frontline

Spinward Fringe Broadcast 5: Fracture

Spinward Fringe Broadcast 6: Fragments

The Expendable Few: A Spinward Fringe Novel

Spinward Fringe Broadcast 7: Framework

Spinward Fringe Broadcast 8: Renegades

Spinward Fringe Broadcast 9: Warpath

Spinward Fringe Broadcast 10: Freeground

Spinward Fringe Broadcast 10.5: Carnie's Tale

Spinward Fringe Broadcast 11: Revenge

Spinward Fringe Broadcast 12: Invasion

Spinward Fringe Broadcast 13: Warriors

Spinward Fringe Broadcast 14: Rebel

FANTASY

Highshield

Brightwill

NEM: Awakening

HORROR

Dark Arts

www.RandolphLalonde.com

Thank you for supporting the author by purchasing this book. Every honest reader counts.

Revision 3

EBook ISBN: 978-1-988175-06-5

Paperback ISBN: 978-1-988175-51-5

PROLOGUE

Year 998.4 United Core Authority Calendar
The Basic Era

HUMANITY IS SLOWLY RECOVERING from a galactic holocaust. After a virus that turned artificial intelligences against them ravaged the population and reduced centuries old systems of law and order to mere memory, the once civilized core worlds have become mostly lawless territory. Mostly.

The United Core Authority discovered a tool, a new virus they began using to prevent artificial intelligences from communicating with other computer systems digitally, reducing their effectiveness and turning the tide of the war. Along with a campaign to neutralize advanced technology that is not under their control, they have managed to quiet the open war that threatened to end humanity in a growing group of solar systems.

New wars begin, some driven by artificial intelligences who

have become trapped in single metal chassis, others conducted by humans with grand ideas and too much hardware. Any spacer will tell you that the conflict map changes daily, and while that provides opportunity for some, it is also a constant source of danger.

Slavery is the fastest growing industry now that mankind has lost trust in intelligent machines. People of all ages run the risk of being captured and sold if they are caught alone in the streets. The drive to reclaim technology that was once used to create enhanced and custom humans is on. There are examples of this golden age of human production from before the Holocaust, when artificial intelligences turned on their masters. They were made from entirely synthetic reproductive materials, customized to have restricted life spans and unrestricted potential. They are called dolls.

Some of them were able to escape during the Holocaust, others remain in service to their masters, but they are all highly sought after since the laboratories and other facilities responsible for their creation are surrounded by armies led by artificial intelligences that will do anything to prevent humanity from getting their hands on the tools for progress in the Geist System.

Through this, the elements of humanity that were already used to hiding – criminals and the ultra-wealthy – have thrived in their own ways. The difference between the two have become only skin deep, and they control the spaces where humanity tries to thrive. Both sides are ruthless in their quest to be in power when order is restored, while the United Core Authority operates as a military dictatorship on the few worlds they can afford to police regularly.

After saving everyone she could and winning her freedom

from her old master, the Countess, Spin Dunewell begins her search for a safe place where they can catch their breath, gather the money they earned from ransoming members of the Countess' court, and buy or steal a ship that will be more difficult for their enemies to trace. All the while, some of Spin's friends are growing more focused on getting revenge on Captain White for betraying them to the Core Authority. That is a goal that could put them in more danger and complicate Spin's plan to gear up and run.

ONE

The weapon had become an artefact. Objectively, it was a nice gun, with well-polished metal surfaces, a brute spinning cylinder inside another atop a trigger and handle. The clip carried only fourteen rounds. It should seem like just another object in the bottom of Spin's bag, but it was the weapon that murdered Larken.

A few of those engineered frack rounds spun from its barrel, broke apart and put great big holes in his torso. She could have put him in stasis with medication if another one hadn't ricocheted and torn through the back of his head. That should have been the end, but he was just conscious enough to look her in the eye, tell her how much he loved her, that she should move on, and then he died in unimaginable agony, squeezing her hand and grinding his teeth together so hard that she could hear the squeak of the enamel.

That weapon reminded her of his last moments. When she thought of him, tried to reach those happy memories, those blood soaked minutes got in the way. She could only see him suffering. The weapon was an artefact, it had become something special, unique. No other thing in the universe had done what that had done.

"Retiring the shredder?" asked Sun as she leaned into the doorway of the quarters Aspen had borrowed for their two-day journey.

"Just saving it for a special occasion," Spin replied. "I found a multiplier pistol in the arms locker. There wasn't much else in there, a few stunners, a bandolier of EMP grenades and a dermal printer."

"High res or?"

"High resolution enough to print new dermal computers, communication links, and whatever else. I already printed a comlink on my jaw. Can you see it?" Aspen asked.

Sun took a look at where Spin pointed at her right jawline. "I can't see it at all, it blended right in."

"I doubt all but the best scanners could pick it up. We'd better keep the printer away from Nigel, or he'll burn it out adding display surfaces to his skin."

"Good thinking, he's already got two comlinks printed somewhere on his face, and both his forearms are stitched up with intelligent displays, so he doesn't need any more upgrades."

"He got the other arm done?" Spin asked.

"Yeah, and most of his back."

"I never understood the need to get a display surface printed into your back. You're the only one who can't see it."

"Ah, he's just a modder junkie, like those people with tattoos in old holos and period flicks."

"I guess so," Spin said. "We're almost in the Diori System?"

"Yeah, a few minutes from emergence," Sun replied. "I've been meaning to ask, are you okay? I heard who Larken was to you, Della told me about it last night. You never talked about him."

"I thought I did. I thought I told you about him. Doesn't matter, when I was on the Cool Angel, I was sure he was dead," Spin said. "I took over a year to move on, and even then I thought about him every day. Less, you know how it is, but still, every day."

"I don't really know how it is, he was like your other half, wasn't he?" Sun asked. "You've also been off on your own a lot, and sleeping half the day."

"I took something, it's taken care of, at least for another three weeks. The sleeping, well, I've mostly been thinking, dreaming." More like brooding, preparing, Spin thought. "Running a lot of katas, doing a lot of yoga to clear my head."

"You don't have to do it alone," Sun said. "And you shouldn't take more of that stuff. Those drugs are for the worst cases, catatonia, constant panic attacks, hypervigilance and delusions."

"When I took that little pill my mind had stopped. I hated everything around me so much that I almost spaced Mirra and Della along with the body of the pilot who killed Larken. Della's tears brought me back to my senses just enough to stop me from doing something horrible, and Mirra calmed me down enough to start thinking a few minutes ahead. If it weren't for this drug, I would be curled up in a ball right in that corner, and I bet you'd still be waist deep in toxic sludge."

"Sounds like you owe more to Della and Mirra than to any pill."

"Maybe, but I'd rather take a pill every few weeks to dull my grief for Larken and be as useful as I can be for all the time I have left than spend the rest of my life suffering for the loss." Spin closed her duffel bag and walked past her into the corridor. "I'll be fine. Oh, and if you want to practice anything, just ask. I'm sure the whole crew could use it to clear their heads." She continued on to the stairs leading up to the cockpit where Nigel watched the scanners.

"That's not the point, everyone wants to support you while you get through this."

Spin turned and faced Sun at the top of the stairs. "I'm fine. I can't see what anyone could do to help. The meds take the edge off; I can focus on what's important. When I'm not busy with that, I can mope and feel sorry for myself in private."

"Um, coming out of FTL in a few seconds here," Nigel said, getting out of the pilot's seat. "I'll fly this thing if you want, but I'm no pilot."

"No worries, we were finished," Spin said as she dropped into the chair. "I'll take the controls, Sun's distracted by my lack of wailing and whining."

"I think I'll go see if our passengers are ready to go," Nigel said, hastily escaping from the cockpit.

"I'm just watching out for you," Sun said. "If you say you're all right, then okay, but if you need someone to help you through this, I'm here."

"Okay, got it," Spin said. The Fleet Feather emerged from the wormhole and new sensor information was added to the pre-emptive scans that were already under way. Their destination,

Gena Station, was only minutes away. "It's an old colony ship," Spin said. "Shouldn't we be picking up energy readings at this distance though? Maybe some port traffic?"

"Yeah, Genna's always busy," Sun said, adjusting the scanners. "There are usually hundreds of ships around. There's usually an old British Alliance carrier around too, it's the main defence."

Spin increased the range of their scans as she and Sun watched the results come in. There was some wreckage spread across thousands of kilometres, but no active ships or buoys.

"This isn't bad, it's whoa-crazy bad," Nigel called up from below. "I'm watching the scanners, and I'm only picking up basic life support on the station. There are no ships around it, a holy-fuck-ton of damage to the port side, and a few cargo containers tucked in to an open section."

"Is that a metric holy-fuck-ton, or an Issyrian standard measure holy-fuck-ton?" Sun asked as she scanned through the data.

"Either way, I don't think your boy Quino or his people are here. If they are, they must have gotten slagged along with whoever was unlucky enough to see this go down first hand," Nigel said.

"The scrambling field is still up," Sun said. "Just enough signal noise to make small life signs inside impossible to pinpoint. There could be scavengers aboard, we wouldn't be able to see unless there were thirty, maybe forty of them in a small area."

"I'm sure there are," Spin said. "If those containers weren't sign enough, there are still computers in there," Spin said. "Navigational guidance computers, small ones. Our antenna's picking a few of them up, so the cherry pickers and bigger outfits probably haven't found this place yet."

"Excuse me," asked a female voice from below. "We aren't going there, are we? From what I'm overhearing, it sounds bad."

It was one of their less useful passengers, a young woman who was sent to the work camp by the Countess as a punishment. Spin hadn't taken the time to get to know most of them, especially since they were only waiting, eating their food and breathing their air until they reached a somewhat civilized port. "Della," Spin said into her comm.

"Wow, your new communicator's nice and clear. Yes, Spin?"

"Can you make sure our passengers are comfortable?"

"Miss? Are we going there? It sounds dangerous?" the woman at the bottom of the stairs pressed.

Della was there a few seconds later. "Don't worry, they know what they're doing. Just have a seat and we'll tell you what we're doing once we know for sure, okay?"

"I'm just," the woman stammered. "I have to contact my brother, you know, he'll want to know what the Countess did to me. He'll need to know where I am so he can come for me."

"I know. We'll get to civilization soon."

Sun shook her head and leaned away from the scanner displays. "There's maybe a handful of people in there, the scramblers keep me from finding out where, but we won't be alone if we go aboard."

"This may be worth checking though," Spin said. "If I can get one or two of those navigational nodes, the small ones, I could use them to make new hardware transponders. Maybe even add a security layer to our next ship."

"That could save us hundreds of thousands of credits," Sun said. "But I don't want to take too much of a risk. I'm thinking we should move on, leave the vultures to pick at this."

"We just get aboard quick, run for the nearest node, pull one, maybe two of the smallest computers, and run back." The converted colony ship came into view. It was over three kilometres long and two wide with nearly three hundred decks. "We'll do a close pass with the Fleet Feather, try to get past their scramblers and then dock where we don't see scavengers. If this was an official claim..."

"There would be a buoy announcing it," Sun said. "So they're not supposed to be here either."

"Right. So, we might need the tech if we want to make our next ship untraceable, are we getting it?"

Sun thought for a moment, looking at the large grey and green station that filled the cockpit window. "We split up, give ourselves half an hour and bug out."

"An hour, I know we can get some serious tech in one hour. The more we bring to the table when we meet someone who we can trade this ship in to, the better."

"All right, an hour," Sun said. "No risks, if any of us run into armed opposition, we get back here and move on. We'll have to land somewhere in the Diori system to drop our passengers off and ask about Quino, see if his people got off the station."

"Sounds good to me," Spin said, leaving the pilot's seat. "You're the better pilot."

"We'll have to do something about that," Sun said, sitting down. "You need more practice."

"I'll get it."

TWO

It was like a race, with Nigel, Sun and her all running through the corridors on the starboard side of the station. They stayed away from the control centre and engineering, that is where they'd find serious scavengers. They all took different corridors so they could get as much as possible then get out. "I got one!" Sun said over their encrypted channel.

"What? It's only been five minutes!" Nigel replied. "I'm going deeper, going to find a real jackpot, I bet there's even a store in this section."

"Just get the navigational nodes, they'll be worth a lot more than anything you find in a store," Spin said as she skidded to a stop in front of a panel. There was a node right behind it, cheerily announcing the location, spin rate, trajectory, and other essential data to any systems that would listen. A station that size needed that kind of technology to keep itself together, and to make managing it much easier for the administration. Why they used such high quality components for a simple task was beyond Spin, but from the looks of the darkened corridors, everything in the converted colony ship was top of the line. As she pried the access panel loose and started detaching the palm sized, sealed computer from its interface cables, she wished that she'd had a chance to see the station in its prime. "Got one," she said as the last cable came loose. The computer kept running for several seconds before it powered down. "This one's in an impact case, like a black box."

"Mine was too, whoever had this ship built spent more money than all of us have ever seen put together," Sun said. "This place is going to be crawling with vultures like us in no time."

"Going down a few levels, may be out of comm range for a few minutes, see you back on the ship," Nigel said.

"Don't go too far, Nigel, these aren't worth getting left behind for," Sun said. "Nigel? God dammit, he's already out of range."

"Ooh, my node had a backup," Spin said as she pried a second one loose and disconnected it.

Navigational nodes, or complex micro-quantum computers of the class that were scattered across Genna Station were becoming more difficult to find all the time. No human could effectively ensure that one was made properly on the assembly line, it took complex computing to make them, the kind of computing that artificial intelligences were responsible for before they went rogue. Sure, humans would eventually develop software that could do the same job, but that could take decades.

There was a CMQC at the heart of every ship that served as a genuine, unique transponder, and as long as Spin had the hardware, she could program a convincing fake. If she could bribe an official to enter a fake transponder built with one of those, it would become as good as real, with records backing it up. The thought of having a ship with more than one transponder so they could hide in plain sight made her want to make the hour she had to loot as many of the Genna Station's navigational nodes as possible. If they could get more than three, they could easily wipe out the data on them and sell the hardware as high-end blanks.

"Running to the next one," Spin said as she sprinted down the hallway. Genna Station's gravity, air recyclers and heaters were all still running, and she couldn't figure out why. On a whim, she linked the computer printed on her arm to the next service panel through her suit. "Um, Sun? The station says that emergency self-repair systems are running. That's why life support is back up." She opened her headgear and let it slide into the pocket between her shoulders. "The air even smells clean."

"That's nice, did you get the next node? We don't have time for sightseeing."

"Okay fine, grabbing this node and moving on," Spin said. "I almost feel bad though, it's not like the station will miss a couple dozen of these, there are hundreds throughout, but if a few more scavengers go after the nodes, there could be trouble."

"The next crime lord who takes this place can worry about that. It's not like this place was home to the finest people in the galaxy," Sun said.

"You have a point," Spin said as she dropped another pair of nodes into her hip pocket. "That's four for me."

"I have five, we might just call it quits soon and retreat while the getting's good. We're already ahead of what we thought we'd get."

"And that's not including whatever Nigel is into right now." Spin ran down the hallway, chasing a bright blip on her scanner that told her that the next node, or pair of nodes were several hundred metres down the long corridor. "Still, I'd rather make use of the whole hour, who knows how much we'll find if we risk just a little." The sounds of her thigh-high boot's heels clacking against the deck rang in her ears. The longer she used the things, the more she hated them. Finding some sensible boots was starting to become a priority.

She slowed to a walk for a few moments to catch her breath, admiring the thick transparent metal hull to her left. The view of the stars with little light to interfere was stunning. The brightest part of the galaxy shone before her eyes, a luminescent cloud of stars. For the first time, thinking of Larken, and how she wished he could be seeing that with her didn't only sadden her. She knew him well enough to imagine an expression of wonder. Out of the two of them, he was the one inspired by visual things, and this would have sent his imagination on a wonderful tangent. "I'll see the sights for both of us."

"What's that, Aspen?" Sun asked.

"Nothing, just took a minute to catch my breath," Spin replied, turning towards the corridor that would lead her to at least one node. A four way split in the hallway was coming up. Her scanner beeped a warning as she noticed something move in the darkness, and drew her sidearm as her boots failed to get a good grip on the deck. Spin slid to a stop, still on her feet, brandishing her sidearm at a thickly muscled short man carrying a massive rifle. He aimed it at her, his eyes wide with surprise and stopped as he realized that she'd beaten him to it, and already had her weapon pointed at his head. "Don't move," she said, noticing that he had a taller, much bigger friend to his left.

To her right, the shadows seemed to move in the gloom, and someone in a heavy helmet drew her weapon, pointing it at the largest of the group. "This is definitely not where I saw myself ending up today. Standoffs with three strangers are not on my list of favourite things," Spin said, holding her inertial multiplier sidearm – a vicious looking thing with a five-centimetre-wide pulse emitter on the front – as steady as she could. She loved seeing a standoff in entertainment. The tension, the suspense, and at the end of every great standoff, someone always fired, setting the whole thing off. It was her first time being in one for real, and she was quickly gaining an understanding of the real danger, hoping for a very different ending than the one she usually cheered for.

"What? Did you say you're in a standoff, Aspen?" Sun asked through her comm. Spin was very happy her question couldn't be overheard.

"I'm Spin, just passing through," Spin said. "Leaving, in fact, unless someone has something to say about it."

"I might," the short, muscled rifle bearer said. There was something familiar about his voice.

"I'm coming, I have you on my locator," Sun said.

The tallest of them twitched his weapon to the left, so it was aiming at the helmeted comer, who flicked her pistol's aim at him in return. "I am absolutely, positively certain that I do not have a dog in this fight, no grudge with any of you and I don't want what's here enough to lose my head."

"Scavenger?" the rifle bearer said, and from the sound of his voice she finally realized who he was. Lin Shae, an acquaintance of the captain of the Cool Angel.

She didn't answer, but eyed the muzzle of his massive rifle for a moment, her eyes finally adjusting to the scant light. He didn't have any bags with him, neither did his friend, so they weren't here to pick at the bones of the great ship. Did he track her here? Was he moonlighting as a slave hunter?

Her shoulder complained at how long her arm was outstretched holding the inertial multiplier. It was a large weapon for a handgun, but surprisingly light. No, it wasn't the weight of the thing that had her arm aching, it was how long she'd been aiming it at Lin Shae's head.

He had a much more intimidating weapon, a pulse rifle that looked like he'd torn it off the side of some old starfighter. The other two, one who pointed at Lin, the other who pointed at her, she didn't know. One was probably a henchman for Lin, that was the one that pointed at her, he had a blue and green Mohawk and an absent look on his face – she expected him to start drooling any moment. The other, the one who quickly shifted her aim back to Lin, she didn't know, and it didn't seem like Lin knew the woman in the blacked out helmet either. The thing had bars running down the front in a V and from her body armour, Spin guessed it was a woman, but it was hard to tell for sure. It could have been a small man, or a short alien.

"Aspen." Lin said, his forehead creasing in irritation. "Why's a girl like you stealing from a place like this?"

"Why are you here?"

"That's my business," Lin said. "Just unlucky enough for you to catch up with me. Am I wanted dead, or alive?"

Spin's confusion only deepened as she realized that Lin thought she was tracking him.

"This suspense is killing me, why don't we blast it out and see whose armour is better?" asked Lin.

"I have the best armour, question answered," said the dark helmet. It waved its plasma blaster from Lin, to Spin, to the Mohawk, who actually looked a little intimidated for a quarter second, then back to Lin.

"I'm almost there," Sun said through the comlink she had buried in her jawbone. "God, this ship's big."

"I'm just waiting to see who tires out first. You brought the biggest gun, Lin. You might be regretting it now, though. Just wondering, why are you on this drifting heap?"

"Salvage, my wrecking crew is going to latch on to this old heap any second now."

"Nothing on scans," Sun said, out of breath from running down a corridor somewhere else in the old colony ship. Hopefully somewhere close. "If he had help coming, they're really late or they're already so close to the station that their location is being hidden by the jammers."

"You never were a good bluffer, Lin," Spin said.

"When did you get a chance to see me gamble?"

"You don't remember playing Seven Star on the Cool Angel? Officer's game?"

"Oh, now I remember, you were serving drinks and slinging snacks, some kind of petty officer." Lin adjusted his grip on his outrageously large rifle.

"Getting a little hard to hold on there, Lin?" Spin asked with a smirk.

"I've got hours left in me, *hours,* don't worry."

"So, who's the guy with the unfortunate haircut?" she asked.

"My nephew," Lin replied. "Boy will do anything for me."

His nephew smiled broadly, nodding, his eyes not quite focusing right.

"Family's important. You know, if you're just doing salvage, I'll just leave you to your work after we get a few parts for our ship. There's someone else here though, their jammers are keeping me from seeing where they are though."

"My handiwork. I say you just move along," Lin said without hesitation.

"We only want a few nav nodes, won't mean anything to your bottom line." Spin said.

"Okay, fine. Did you just come here for salvage? Most people don't even know this place was abandoned yet."

"Actually we were looking for Quino, this used to be his place, right?"

"Well, yeah, he shared with a couple other outfits, but not for about nine months. He moved on to Wayland Prime, running an even bigger operation there."

"So, you'll put that down if I promise to grab a couple parts and move on?" Spin said.

"Well, yeah," Lin said.

"Then why did you draw on me?"

"You drew on me first, remember?" Lin asked. "Why is that, anyway?"

"You surprised me, besides, don't you hunt slaves as a side business?"

"No, we used to bounty hunt before the 'bots went crazy and cut up their humans. You know, tracking murderers, big ticket thieves, no slaves though. That's shit-heel work, thug bullshit."

"So, we're all right here, and he's your kin," Spin said. "So, who's this helmet whose pointing her weapon at you?"

Lin glanced at her, then back to Spin, his eyes widening. "Fuck."

"Do you remember Marli Owen's daughter, Terry?" a garbled female voice asked from the black helmet.

"Oh, shit, he took a hit out on me for that?"

"No, you idiot, I'm her, I'm Terry. You didn't even leave a note. I've been tracking you for three weeks."

"Didn't recognize you in the combat armour, how ya been?" Lin asked, trying to sound casual.

Spin lowered her sidearm and dropped it into her thigh holster.

"You gave me the grish. It's in stage two."

Spin's jaw dropped. "Oooooh," Sun and Nigel said over their channel, she could practically hear the pair of them cringing. Of all the sexually transmitted diseases to catch, the grish was the worst. It remained dormant in its first stage, spreading to partners with little trace. Stage two resulted in painful internal and external sores that dripped pus. It took months to treat in that stage, and if you didn't catch it in time, it would move on to phase three, the flesh eating phase.

Lin's nephew looked shocked, glancing from Lin to the helmeted woman over and over again.

"Oh my God," Sun said over the communicator. "I almost slept with him last year. Bullet dodged. But, hey, we could make a friend here."

"A friend who will have us cleaning chairs and toilet seats

every time he visits," Nigel said. "What did I just start hearing? I just got back into range."

"Never mind, we'll catch you up later," Sun said.

"At least you're not pregnant?" Lin told Terry with a shrug.

The sound of a loose panel somewhere down the dark corridor made everyone flinch. The corridor intersection was flooded with bright light as the helmeted former lover fired. Spin understood what Sun was getting to, they could make an ally – if a sleazy one – out of Lin. Even though Spin thought he deserved what he had coming, at least a little, she leapt at the armoured woman, tackling her to the ground.

To her surprise, Terry batted her hard enough to knock the wind out of her and send her sliding more than a dozen metres down the hallway. As soon as she started to slow down, Spin rolled into a side corridor, a short range plasma bolt narrowly missing her.

The nephew took the opportunity and opened fire on the helmeted woman, peppering her with blazing energy shots until she was a heap on the floor. "Everything okay, Spin?" Sun asked.

"I got clear, and Terry the dark helmet girl is a hot pile. Don't know about Lin, I'm going to check now," Spin said as she rushed back to the hall intersection.

"Good, I'm one hatch away, but have to cut through."

"I'll be here." Spin was already reaching into her jacket for her emergency patch kit.

"Fuck, that was my good arm," Lin groaned as he laid on his intact side. The stump of his right arm was a burnt mess, and there wasn't enough of the arm left to reattach. "Thanks for slagging that bitch, Jon."

"You kinda had it coming," Spin said as she knelt down with a tension patch. "This is going to hurt like crazy before the medication kicks in." Lin screamed as she stretched it over his stump and it conformed to the end, wrapping the wound up to his shoulder and affixing itself tightly.

Jon, who was carefully prying the helmet off Terry's head, only spared his screaming uncle a short glance.

"Okay, the meds are kicking in," Lin said, panting. "You didn't have anything that you could have given me first?"

"Sure I did, but I thought you deserved some misery for passing the grish around, I mean, seriously, who doesn't use protection these days? It's not like there's a clinic on every corner."

"I lost a fucking arm and you're giving me shit about not sealing up before getting it up?" Lin asked.

Jon laughed, it was a low, breathy sound. "This might fit you," he said as he offered the helmet to Spin.

Spin looked at it and at the woman on the deck. The only thing not reduced to a burnt pile of human remains was her face, which was twisted in an expression of fury and pain. "Thank you, Jon," she said. "I think I'll clean it before trying it on though."

"We'll be going back to the ship," Lin groaned. "Jon, get my quad blaster."

Jon did so, then pried Lin's disembodied hand off the handle and offered it to him.

"Don't think there's enough arm to put that back on, buddy," Lin said.

"Wait, you're not going to wait for your scavenging ship? Maybe they could take care of you."

"I'll fess up. We're scouting for Kiren Arms. I was just taking a run through the ship here to see if there were any high end trinkets we could grab before we reported this gold mine. I thought we'd have a good payday coming, but it looks like I'll be spending it all on a new arm."

"And some serious anti-fungal treatments," Sun said as she emerged from a side passage. Like Spin, she was in a thick, form-fitted containment suit, only hers was dark red. Her white jacket was armoured, but not quite as well made as Spin's, which was black and had a refractive coating on top that made it seem darkly multi-coloured.

"What? Is the Cool Angel right behind?" Lin said.

"No, we broke away from that crew a while ago," Sun replied. "You've seen better days."

"You're not here because of some unrequited thing, are you? Already had one former sex-type-thing track me down today."

"Absolutely not," Sun said emphatically. "We just bumped into you by luck. We had no idea there was anyone else aboard."

"Speaking of which, there are pickers aboard, I've been avoiding them for hours, and my knees are getting a little wobbly. The meds are doing me a lot of good, so I should get back to the ship. Take whatever you can carry, it'll be two days before we report this thing as abandoned and a salvage crew dig in."

"We'll help you to your ship if you or your nephew tell us all about the places a few people who want to avoid the law may do business. We're looking for a safe harbour to operate out of, and someone who will trade with people trying to avoid the law. Someone who won't turn an escaped slave in."

"Sure thing," Lin said. Jon picked his uncle up, a feat that seemed easy even though he was only slightly larger than him. "I'll even set you up with our ident, so you can call us up later. You know, in case you need anything, or want to get together."

"Thanks," Sun said. "But just business."

"Sure, just don't share what happened here, I have a reputation."

"No problem, the more you share, the less we'll share," Spin said.

"Deal."

THREE

"All right, Nigel's in," Della announced with a giggle towards the cockpit door. Sun made sure the airlock was secure then detached from the station. She let the Fleet Feather drift fifteen meters from the base before activating the thrusters and putting the derelict behind them.

"We'll be good to make our next wormhole jump as soon as you get us clear," Spin said. She was looking over the information that Lin had given them. "He really gets around. Five ports in three days, two of them off UCA's scanners."

"That's a start. Did he give us any information that'll help us get in touch with Quino?"

"Well, Wayland Prime is a 'junk pit' according to his personal log entry on it. The UCA carpet bombed the place with EMP emitters and conventional warheads then left the planet for dead almost a year ago. There are a few cities though, it says the Red River Rippers, or Rippers are Quino's new outfit, they're in – you guessed it - Red River Province."

"Quino was never very original, but he was also never a slaver. Well, unless you owed him money, then you could work it off. I made sure I never owed him anything," Sun said.

"Well, there are a lot of escaped slaves there, I'm thinking there are some slave hunters running around too though."

"Where there's one, there will be the other. Could a bounty notice from the Countess reach that far already?"

Spin checked the sector map and guessed how far the transmission containing their bounties had spread, if there was one. "If she transmitted as soon as I escaped, it would take at least another few days to get there using hyper-transmitters. Unless the UCA has repaired everything along the route, which is unlikely, then it could get there today."

"Here's hoping they were busy elsewhere," Sun said. The Fleet Feather slipped into the wormhole and she engaged the autopilot. "Let's see what Nigel got his hands on. Thankfully, we won't have to depend on his loot."

Nigel was already holding court in the small galley. Most of their passengers filled the dozen seats, including Mirra and Della. On his head was a crown made of lollipops and sweet veggie snacks that was held together by their loudly coloured, interconnected plastic packaging.

Around his neck he'd strung chocolate medallions with snack bags and drink pouches. He finished dumping the contents of the backpack he filled on the station, revealing more snacks and a wealth of low-cost, low quality novelty items.

A few of the passengers sat back with their arms folded, obviously thinking they were above the convenience store junk. Mirra shook her head but couldn't help but smile at Nigel as he handed her a green sour pop. "I'm going to make a guess here, that your favourite flavour is green apple. Careful, it's so sour your face might pull itself inside out."

"Thank you, not big on green apple, but I love sour," she said as she accepted the pop.

"I'm taking these if no one wants them," Della said, laughing as she pulled a box of disposable thongs from the pile. "There's one missing?" she asked as she examined the broken seal.

"I can assure you that they are very comfortable," Nigel said with a grin. "I'm wearing one right now!" His audience erupted, mostly with laughter, but a few recoiled, unimpressed with the mental image.

"Oh, so you'd rather we share?" Della asked.

"Nah, I think they're more your style," Nigel said. "And for our Governor," he said, passing him a long string of chocolate coins in golden foil. "You should dress that consuit up with something."

The Governor stood and bowed his head so Nigel could put it on him. "Normally only Mayors in my territory wore chains of office, but I thank you, the British Alliance and her territory of New Parisia thanks you."

"You're welcome," Nigel said as the Governor fixed him with a warm smile and shook his hand firmly.

"Now for something more serious," Nigel said, pulling a medical hand scanner from the pile. "Got a couple of these, one should go to our medic."

Leland, who was only a little shorter if you didn't include a wild, tall head of dark hair that shot straight up from his head, accepted the pair of new hand scanners. "Wow, I couldn't afford this brand, thanks. I'll put one in medical."

Spin watched as Sun took that as her opportunity to make her announcements. "Sorry to interrupt, but I thought you'd all like to know we're headed to an active port. It's off the map, but they'll most likely have working long range communications, transport so you can get to where you're going, and shops that can provide what you need. I don't expect we'll be there long."

"What about our slave marks?" asked Tamara, one of the formerly wealthier slaves they'd rescued. "There could be hunters there."

"From what we could figure out knowing that a lot of the data hyper-nodes are still out of operation, so slave hunters don't have your information yet, but you can expect to be on wanted lists as they update throughout the sector. You can either run or contact someone you trust like family members, your oldest friends, people who have a real incentive to make sure you stay free and hidden. Please only reveal your next location, not where we land."

"What's the place we're going called?"

"Mi Sao, a port city on Wayland Prime. It's in Red River Province. We know someone there who may help this ship and crew."

"That was in the nullified zone," one of their passengers said. Spin had to check with her manifest to remember his name, Colin Drey, he was enslaved by the Countess' people when they were on patrol around the operation they rescued him from. "Listen, I'm an all right electrician and can help with just about anything around the ship, can I just sign up with your crew?"

"Is it that bad?" Tamara asked, wide eyed. "The place we're going?"

"Not if you can buy passage off to a place that'll take you, they've got transport there, for sure. I'm just so far from my people that I'd never make it, and I'd rather stick with this crew if they're going to put a hurt on House Bridgewater, the Countess and her grandson have it coming."

Sun looked to Spin who nodded. "If you can contribute, you can join the crew, but we're going to be monitoring all your transmissions. If you're caught jeopardizing anyone's freedom, I'll space you myself."

"Oh, and we're not continuing on this ship," Sun added. "Whatever we end up on won't be nearly as posh. What we're going after won't be big profit stuff. This trip is about staying free, and we're going to look for a way for Aspen – sorry, I mean, Spin, to stay alive past her expiration date. That could mean we go to some dangerous places."

Spin was surprised to hear the announcement. "I don't want to put anyone through what that could take. I don't even know if it's possible."

"I'm going to make that happen for you," Sun said. "And anyone who isn't with me on that shouldn't sign up for the crew."

Nigel pulled his crown of goodies off and surrendered his necklaces to the middle of the table. "Yeah, that's gotta happen. I want to see Captain White dead, the governor here back where he belongs, and maybe get some payback on the Countess and her house, but most of all, I'd hate to see you die before your time, Spin. Boro said something, you know, when we were in the swamp. He said he couldn't find something he didn't like about you, and you know, I couldn't either. People like that should be around. Should be around for a long time."

"I'll help however I can," Governor Dantor said. "Keep in mind, I probably won't be able to get my post back, but I may still have connections. I won't be able to stay on the ship for long, depending on what I'll have to do."

"If you can be more service to your people by leaving, then I'd rather know you're helping thousands of people rather than just me," Spin said.

"Millions," Tamara said. "He's not a regional governor, he's a planetary governor."

"Then you definitely have to go if you can help them."

"Thank you for your leave, young lady," Governor Dantor said with a little impish smile. "But I'll make that decision for myself. I'll help on the ship with information and whatever I'm qualified for while I figure out what my next best move is, if you'll have me."

"No one has to decide right away. We have a few hours before we get to Wayland Prime," Sun said. "Nigel, can I speak to you out here for a minute?"

He retreated from the galley and stepped outside. Sun closed the door. "Listen, I understand that you wanted to have a little fun while you got some time off ship, but we were there to gather valuable technology, something that everyone would value from port to port."

"I couldn't find more than a medical centre that was already scraped bare, except for a couple scanners someone tucked back on the top shelves. Then I ran into a convenience kiosk on the way out and thought I'd load up."

"On junk?" Sun asked.

"Morale boosters," Nigel said, the pace of his speech picking up rapidly as he explained himself. "I know we've got the best of the best on this ship, the cupboards have food in them I've never even seen before, but what I brought back is exciting, look at it, it's like a colour explosion happened on that table, and I think everyone we care about is having a laugh. We needed that, you know, because that plantation was fucking terrifying, we all thought that was it for us, we gotta forget."

Sun smiled at him a little. "I get it, and those medical scanners are a big deal, I've never seen one of that quality at close range. In the future, stick to the plan and stay in communications range, okay? We'll have time to raid abandoned stores every once in a while."

"All right, no problem," he replied. "There's something I've gotta tell you though. I've been spending a lot of time with our passengers, half of them should be crew, and they want to be. I bet they'll stick around even if they know it's not about the money. There are others, though, like Tamara and her friend, they're going to burn us. The moment they can send a message home, I just know they're going to trade our location to get back in with their people, or maybe just because they think their rescuers should have come in on a white horse or something. It's like we're not good enough to lend a helping hand, and they're just a bunch of greedy fuckers."

"Point them out to me, and we'll leave them on Wayland Prime to fend for themselves," Sun said.

"After giving them a couple hundred pips so they're not completely helpless," Spin added. "I'm not going to drop them in the middle of a lawless port with no cash, even if they're all going to screw us over."

"A couple hundred pips?" Nigel asked. "Are we wealthy or something? What did you guys get on that station?"

"After a misunderstanding we were able to finish our raid and we made off with thirty-five programmable complex-micro quantum computers, they were using them as navigational nodes, the ones we said you should grab."

"What? They were using that kind of tech for something a bunch of old Pinewoods could do? Little computers you could find anywhere?"

"I guess they decided quality was king when the parts were still cheap and plentiful," Sun said.

"That haul's worth a couple hundred grand, probably more," Nigel said. "Now I feel bad for stopping for a corner store kiosk. They didn't even have anything really good left. I mean, even I have to admit my haul is mostly junk, just enter-taining junk."

"Well, you may as well get back in there and enjoy it," Sun said. "Your morale boosting seems to be working."

"Yeah?"

"Go have some fun, make them forget about where they've been for a few hours," she said.

"You two have gotta join in," he said. "C'mon."

"Maybe later," Spin said, eying the door to the small infirmary.

"I have to monitor the ship from the cockpit," Sun said. "Next time."

"You'd better," Nigel said as he rejoined the already mellowing crowd in the galley.

"He's handling things well," Spin said.

"He's hiding, but I think it's his way," Sun said. "How are you doing?"

"I'm all right. I think it's time to let Larken's body go. We'll be passing close to the Wayland system's star on the way. We should stop for a moment so I can," Spin trailed off, Sun was already nodding so she didn't have to explain what she wanted to do.

"Celeste is a beautiful star, it's a good place to send him," she said.

"I don't want to do anything, just say goodbye one last time, so it won't take long."

"Are you sure?" Sun asked, concern deeply etched on her face.

Spin nodded. "You should get to the cockpit. I'm going to visit." She didn't wait for Sun's response, she was already tired of her concern. Half the people on the ship looked at her as though they expected her to burst into tears at any moment, but that wouldn't happen. It couldn't happen. Between the medication she took that put a filter between her and her sharper emotions so she could begin to cope, and the fact that she didn't have the physical ability to create tears of grief, fear or sorrow, it wasn't possible.

Before she realized it, Spin's hand was resting on the foot of Larken's capsule. The log there said that Leland, their new Medical Technician had accessed it hours before. Without thinking, she opened the top half so she could see Larken's body, and was astounded. He'd been dressed in a white suit that even had a matching jacket.

His hair had been washed, his face cleaned, and the illusion of life had been restored. Even Larken's expression looked peaceful. "I'm sorry, I thought it was a good idea to clean him and Trevor up last night, but I think I've overstepped instead," Leland said as he entered the room.

"No," Spin said, wondering if the medication she was on was working at all. The mixture of grief and strange happiness at seeing him whole, unwounded again, was nearly overwhelming. In one charitable act a person she barely knew, Leland, had given her the opportunity to create a final memory of the person she loved most in the universe. Larken was there, at peace, the hint of a forthcoming smile at the corners of his mouth, and she might remember him like that instead of in pain, gripped by a fear of dying. She took a shuddering breath and stared into Larken's handsome face, the only sign that he was deceased was the utter stillness of him. "Thank you, this is good."

"When I was training I worked for a few morticians, a truly gifted group. I did what I could for Larken with what I had. I couldn't sleep anyway."

He lightly touched her on the shoulder and she turned towards him, where she was caught in an embrace. Leland stroked her back gently, comforting, and she realized that she was shaking. "It's going to be all right," he said to her.

At first she couldn't help but think that he was wrong, entirely wrong. Spin was designed to be a part of a pair, and Larken was the other half of that. There were other Larken's, but they wouldn't match her and they would have their own other half. She would never have that feeling with someone again. Leland didn't offer any more words, just patience and his embrace.

Time passed, and she began to find her own understanding

of his words. It was probably true, she would be all right, she thought Larken was dead before, and it took a long time, but she started to move on. So, her understanding changed, and she allowed herself to concede that things would be all right, but they would never be the same.

Spin stepped away from Leland slowly. "Thank you," she said.

"No problem," he replied. "I know a bit about pairing. I used to work at a shop that would gene-match couples. They'd come in with love in their eyes, and I'd set up minor modification meds to make them an even closer match than they were. Physiologically, at least."

"Did that work?"

"A lot of people swore by it, but we had repeat customers. You know, people who got matched to someone, then they discovered that the physical bond didn't make up for their personalities. We had two escaped dolls while I was there, sorry for using the term, they weren't as rare as you two, but we were able to break the matching."

"Why did they want to be separated? Larken and I were always happiest when we were together, I can't imagine wanting to break that coding."

"They had to," Leland said. "If they didn't change, any security scanner in the civilized sectors would immediately recognize them. We tried to re-match them after we changed them enough to hide, but even I could tell something was missing, like nothing we did would recapture the work that was done before they were born."

"That makes a lot of sense to me," Spin said. "People used to watch us together. We were as close as twins, but not related. I suppose there was a romance to our synchronicity."

"Scientific terms for something that doesn't feel anything like science. You loved each other. Some people try to find that with partners over and over again and never do. You two were lucky to have so much time together."

"You just say whatever's on your mind, don't you?" Spin said.

"I'm sorry, sometimes I forget that some people prefer to grieve gently," Leland said. "I'm not good with this sort of thing. I started losing people when I was young, so I'm used to missing people who can never be there, having to depend on myself."

"It's all right," Spin said. "I can't afford to dwell on things, I don't have much time."

"I know, there are millions of people like you who only have a few years or months left because someone built it into their design. I was a part of the New Freedom Movement before The Fall. Not a popular stance in my field. I'm here because I want to find the solution for you and anyone like you."

"So you're a freedom fighter," Spin said with a little smirk.

"I guess I am. I just look at you and him and see people. I suppose I don't have the nerve to think that you're different because of your origins. Issyrians are born in large clutches, and become schools of young that follow their parents around so they can be fed like pilot fish, but are any of their lives less precious because there are so many of them, or because they begin life in such a basic state? I don't think so."

"I've only met one group of issyrians. I wish I had more time to get to know them. They had trouble grasping dry land culture, but they were so excited, and they had a great sense of humour about it."

"I've met a few, but mostly outcasts. Their senses of humour didn't seem as obvious."

"He had a really good time with them," Spin said, looking back to Larken. She still couldn't believe how lifelike he was.

"Why don't you tell me about him? We have a couple hours, I'd like to know more."

"We were the luckiest slaves. They treated us better than anyone, almost as well as royal children. When we were very young – barely out of toddlerhood – we'd cry if they separated us, so they didn't for years. I experienced the first ten years of my life with my hand in his, and the court of the Countess spoiled us whenever they had the chance. We knew we were different from other children, especially since they were almost always cruel to us when they thought no one was looking. We were eleven years old when we saw the information package that the Countess was presented with before we were born, and we realized that we may have been treated better than any slaves in her estate, but we were certainly not free. We were treated well because we were pretty little rare creatures. That was the first time I saw him truly angry. I was furious too, but also afraid because I saw that we would die young before he did. He put his anger aside to comfort me. We were caught looking through the Countess' records and that night she told us every-thing. He just let the words roll over him without reacting unless he was making sure I wasn't too hurt by it all. Until then, we'd never doubted that the Countess loved us. After that, Larken became curious about the outside world. We both served the Countess faithfully, but I think that's where our conditioning to love her blindly began to break. I don't think it was ever trained into us properly anyway, our instructor was always too interested in letting us make our own choices during our educations, but she was one of the best doll teachers, so she had the estate's trust. Larken took every opportunity to learn about the galaxy, and that's what sparked my interest in a broader world."

"What about him?" Leland asked. "What was it like to be beside him?"

The question surprised Spin, almost as much as what came to her mind first. "He could communicate so much without words. We were so aware of each other, the way we were holding hands, or the way one of us was walking, that it was like we had developed a special sense. When we got older he liked being cheek to cheek. We had busy days, but we stole time to dance together, and he had a way of creating a bubble around us, the rest of the universe disappeared. One time we were in the middle of trade negotiations for the estate with Uramma, and I remember being so bored as I prepared the Urammans. I was stuck alone with them, discussing protocol, educating them on how the Countess' companies normally conducted business. I don't know how he knew I was boring myself half to death, but he did, so I started hearing our favourite music through my private comm. No one else could hear it, but it gave me the lift I needed to finish the day and make things seem interesting for the Urammans. It doesn't seem like much, but it was the perfect thing at the perfect time."

"Keep going," Leland said. "This is interesting, I feel like I'm getting to know him a little."

To Spin's surprise, telling stories about Larken became

easier with time. She remembered things that she hadn't recalled in years. Leland listened with interest, and she began to feel better. By the time they arrived in the Wayland System, she was ready to commit Larken's body to space, where he and Trevor would slowly drift towards Celeste, a sun that burned white.

FOUR

The end of the systems check scrolled across Dorian's vision ending with the words:

ALL SYSTEMS NOMINAL
COMBAT OPTIMIZATION COMPLETE

ONE THING still amazed him about his new body more than anything else: he could feel the synthetic muscle in his replacement limbs, the organ replacement package in his chest, and the high charge of his power cells all priming. High nutrient mixtures flowed through his synthetic and real veins, the pulmonary package pushed more highly oxygenated blood through organs that drank it in greedily, and the recently installed pulse emitter batteries drew on the small power plant in his middle, warming up for what he hoped would be a worth-while payoff.

"One more thing," he muttered to himself, drawing a cigar from a compartment in his right leg. It was black, and as thick as his middle finger. With a mental command, his fingers split down the middle, sliding to each side of his hand to provide a port for the heavy pulse emitter in his right arm. He warmed the business end up until it was red hot and used it to light his cigar, puffing great clouds of smoke before taking a long draw.

The drugs in the DICE smokeable flooded his system, making his completely organic brain race. Memories, thoughts, and a sense of hyper awareness that was so intense that he almost wanted to curl up into the foetal position to slow it all down crashed over him. This was DICE, his drug of choice, the kind of mad high he wished he could find when he was still all human, and he embraced it, breathing the smoke in, letting the organ package process it and fill his senses. He could feel every sensor in his body, process every signal from his synthetic nervous system, and make out every mote of dust floating in the tower top alleyway around him.

The filthy alley overlooked a freeway filled with slider vehicles, and the one he was tracking was near. "Coming, it's coming, it's coming," he said as he readied the cable launcher in his left arm. "Brett is going to pay today. Hope you like me now, Captain."

The wedge shaped personal vehicles, narrow single passenger slip bikes, and larger transport trucks moved along the many layered sky lanes at hundreds of kilometres per hour. Complex software, not artificial intelligences controlled the cars at that speed. People were lounging in their little transports, no one would expect someone to attack anyone on a high velocity stretch, that's why his prey wouldn't see him coming.

Closer, Captain Brett Hoket's eight passenger planet hopper was in the stream of traffic that seemed to move a little slower with every puff of his DICE cigar. "Wings, I got wings now, you little bitch," he said as he deployed a pair of multi-directional thrusters he had installed on his back and got them ready to fire. He could feel their heat increase against his synthetic skin, but it was well within limits. The flight guidance system came online and plotted the course between him and his former captain's small ship. He knew that errand vehicle, he'd repaired it and inspected it in his previous life.

"I got wings, and I'm going to catch you!" he shouted as he activated the thrusters on his back and arced from the rooftop alleyway down to the expressway. The guidance system was new, only calibrated once, so it got the speed right, but he was going to slip between the Captain's car and the one ahead. Dorian fired his hair-thin grappling line from his left arm and grinned as it struck right in the middle of the ship's hull and punctured all the way through.

He reeled himself in and landed with his feet firmly planted on either side of the line. All at once he could feel the wind against the synthetic skin on his face, pulling violently at his overcoat, hear the alarms going off inside the car through the sensor on the end of his boarding line, and enjoy the sight of blurred lights all around as they passed between high skyscrapers and lanes of opposing traffic. "Caaaaaptaaaaaiiiin Hooooooket! Your past is heeeeeere!" The cigar had disinte-grated thanks to the high wind, and he swallowed the wet end that remained in his teeth. Nutrient processing systems began to work on it, sending a new rush of chemicals through him. Someone was laughing so loud that he could hear it over the traffic. It was musically maniacal, and as he wondered who it was, and what they were on, he realized it was him. "Oh my fucking God this is the best DICE!"

The shuttle broke from the stream of traffic and headed down between a row of buildings that were in the massive war zone next to the city core. The night was lit by weapons' fire between the field of plastic, metal and concrete towers. Gangs fought for any of a dozen reasons, and they did it on all levels, between dozens of buildings. Refusing to be distracted by the new light show, Dorian knelt down and began cutting a circle in the top of the shuttle with his pulse emitter. It took seconds to make a new door through the thin shuttle armour.

Dorian made eye contact with a terrified woman in a small tube dress as she pointed a stunner at him and he decided to let her shoot him instead of dodging. The stun shot made contact with his synthetic skin and didn't penetrate to the layers below. "Do I look human enough for that to do anything?" he said, laughing as he dropped inside the shuttle. He tossed her to the back of the seating area and smashed his fist through the thin transparent steel partition. His fingers curled around the rough edge of the divider and he ripped the metal away, revealing his prey. "Hello, Captain. It's time to land," he giggled, catching Captain Hoket's neck in his hand from behind. The sizzle of Hoket's skin against his fingers revealed an oversight – the pulse emitter had heated his synthetic flesh up a couple hundred degrees, so Dorian adjusted his grip so he held the back of the man's fancy blue suit instead, but he didn't stop screaming.

"Shut up and land!" Dorian shouted. He waited as long as

he could, a few seconds, for his old Captain to comply before firing his boarding line at the dashboard and using the interface in the end to signal an emergency to the ship.

The lighting inside turned red, and the vessel plotted its own course to the nearest landing pad, decelerating rapidly. Captain Hoket drew his sidearm – a respectable weapon that fired intelligent rounds – but Dorian snatched it from his hand and deactivated it. "Thank you," he said, sliding it into a pocket inside his battered overcoat. "I always liked your taste in guns. What do you think of mine?" he asked, splitting the fingers in his right hand to reveal the smouldering emitter. "Cut right through this tin can, I wonder how it would do on your thick skull?"

"I paid to have you saved, I didn't know Quino would turn you into this," Captain Hoket said. "He said you could serve out your debt if the cost of fixing you up went over what I paid, not that he'd do this." The man was crying, Dorian couldn't help but laugh at the sight of his tears.

"You disbanded the crew and fucked off to Nyja, everyone got their share, even your fucking whipping boy, but I woke up in a chop shop with less meat than some instant dinners and a debt that's about two hundred murders deep."

"I told them you were a ship thief, not a contract killer! I swear! He said you'd be useful."

"I've killed twenty-eight people in the last thirty days, Quino won't trust me to steal so much as a one man slider with all this expensive hardware under my skin. He won't let me out of the city because he's afraid the bomb he built into my chest won't kill me either. Wait, didn't you hear about this? About me? Didn't you check on how your hull cracker was doing after you left him behind?" The business end of Dorian's pulse emitter began to warm up and hum.

"I just got back, I was going to check in, I swear!"

"Bullshit! Make me believe what you say next, motherfucker!"

"All right! I heard and I am on my way off world right now! I just had some business to take care of so I could leave this shithole behind."

The shuttle set down on a platform. Dorian's navigational system told him he was half way up a skyscraper near the middle of the war zone. "Money! Pay my debt to Quino and the Red River Crew so I can at least get off their chain!"

"I have what's in the back, in that box. You can have it," Captain Hoket said, pointing.

Dorian glanced at the back long enough for his scanners to tell him that there was only thirty-five thousand UCA credits inside. "That's not enough." He snatched the Captain's hand and snapped the bone behind his first finger. It made a satisfying snapping sound. There was something about watching Captain Hoket scream and try to free his hand from Dorian's grip that made him feel a little better.

"Everything else is off world or spent. I was just about to get a new crew together so we could start earning again."

"What about your ship? What about the Chimera?" Dorian asked, scanning for the command chip.

"I sold it, I'm here looking for a good rebuild." He must have noticed something in Dorian's expression that warned him about what would happen next, because he urgently pleaded; "No, whatever I can get, I'll give you," as he tried to guard his hand from further abuse.

Dorian smiled as he snapped the middle bone in Captain Hoket's hand and shifted to the next unbroken segment. "What about the Dawn? What about the ship I nearly died saving?"

"Willy took it as his share!"

"Willy is dead," Dorian said, snapping another bone. He waited for Captain Hoket to stop screaming. "Quino had him killed, I don't know why, I was busy getting used to gears and wires instead of blood and guts."

"Then that's it!" Captain Hoket said. "Kill me if you want, but that's all there is unless you let me go off planet and get more money for you from my stash."

"Where's your stash? I'm going to break your arm next."

"Fuck you! You're not worth the whole thing, you're just a port rat from a career port wife!"

"Shouldn't have insulted my mother," Dorian said. He let go of Captain Hoket, pushed the side door open and left. He turned to the pilot hatch and watched Captain Hoket panic for a moment through the transparent aluminium window. He was trying to get the ship out of emergency mode, but he wouldn't have time.

Four lightly armoured gangland warriors were approaching slowly, weapons drawn. Dorian spared a moment to wink at them. "Just finishing some business here then I'm off, boys." He directed his attention at the pilot side hatch and gestured at Captain Hoket, requesting that he open the window. He chuckled as he watched Hoket panic for a few more seconds then punched his hands through the thin armoured door and tore it from its hinges.

Hoket was in his hands and out of the pilot's seat next, and Dorian scanned him carefully. "New emergency medical module, and an upgraded shock circuit in your arm right under your computer. That's some pretty expensive tech, especially since you didn't have to replace your real arm to get it done."

"Dorian! Listen! I'll go get you however much you need to pay to get your freedom back, then come right back. Or I could transfer it to you!"

"There isn't a bank that will trust you within three sectors of here, not since you started robbing them," Dorian replied. "And you'd never come back if I let you go. I know I wouldn't. Well, I can't get anything for a used EMI, so it'll have to be the arm. I might even be able to figure out where your stash is."

"No, Dorian! I didn't know what he'd do!"

"Didn't much care, either," Dorian said as he walked Hoket to the edge of the landing platform. They were twenty-one storeys up. He grasped Hoket's arm firmly and held him out over the dark emptiness. "I'm going to leave your emergency medical implant installed, just in case it can actually save you from this, but I'm pretty sure you'll be a pile of bloody meats for about thirty seconds, then it'll be darkness forever. I'm keeping your arm." Before his former captain could protest, Dorian fired his pulse emitter and separated Hoket's forearm from the rest of him. His high had been slipping away for a few minutes, but there was still enough in him so he could enjoy every millisecond of Captain Hoket's long fall. "Aye, just a pile of bloody meats at the bottom of that fall."

Dorian turned back towards the shuttle, nodding at the gob smacked gang toughs as he crossed the distance. The woman in the back of the ship screamed and retreated the moment he was inside. He ignored her as he opened the credit box and dropped Hoket's forearm inside then closed it back up. "You might want to get in the pilot's seat, the ship should fly you back to wherever you were last if you hit the return button. Or you could stay here and entertain those guys. I'm sure they'd appreciate the company."

Unsure if the woman heard anything he said, Dorian retreated from the car and took flight, his new thrusters propelling him across the sky at speeds only artificial skin and hair could withstand. The auto-medic at the base of his skull began administering anti-inflammatory medication to his brain as the hangover from DICE started to take hold.

A notification scrolled through his mind's eye:

KNOWN IDENTIFICATION NUMBERS IN RANGE:
Nigel Lozel, Sun Dell

HIS SPIRITS ROSE as he set down atop one of the more peaceful skyscrapers to wait until whatever ship was carrying Nigel found its way to a port. It would be good to see a friendly face, even though he had to wonder if Nigel would even recognize him.

FIVE

The disorder and hardships the galaxy had to offer its citizens were as good as fact to Spin, she'd been to megacities that were in the middle of ripping themselves apart before. Her previous experiences still didn't prepare her for the wars surrounding Midtown. A clear column of massive buildings and port rises were peaceful. Landing instructions and proper guidance signals were provided as though the fall of civilization never happened, but everything around it was marked as a no-go zone, and along the edges of the safe zone signs that violence threatened to swallow the middle of the high rise megacity were constant.

From where they landed near the top of the Comtek Port Building, Aspen could see flaming high rises in the distance, and the light of weapons' fire streaking through the night sky. That was kilometers away, but she knew that without Comtek's energy shielding and security systems, they would not be safe.

Most of the people on her ship were leaving, and the

Comtek building was the safest place for them. There were transports coming and going regularly, and accommodations in case they had to stay for a few days. Most of their passengers were used to living under safer conditions, some were even accustomed to having servants. None of them would be happy with where they would be left, but to Spin, the money they were putting in their hands and the place they were leaving them was the best they could do. They were lucky to be treated so well, other people would have flushed the lot of them out the airlock to limit the risk of being betrayed. She'd never admit it, but the thought crossed her mind more than once while she heard some of their passengers complain.

All the more reason why she was happy that Sun, with the help of everyone else who was joining her crew were telling their passengers what they could expect when they disembarked, not to leave the Comtek building, and making sure that they weren't making off with more than the clothes on their back, and twelve hundred United Core World Authority, or UCA platinum each – a small fortune that would get any of them home, even if they wanted to travel to the furthest fringes. Their new medical technician would be scanning each person as they were handed their bag of coins to make sure they didn't take anything extra, and then they'd be on their way.

Before they could disembark, Spin had to meet with whoever the Port Authority were sending to collect the docking fees and ask questions. Instead of covering her face, she decided that the best way to find out if the wanted notice had reached the planet was to reveal herself. The chances that they were ahead of any bounty or notice were high, so there wasn't much risk. Besides, their ship was almost as conspicuous as she was, so there was no point in hiding. Even still, she'd taken precautions.

Looking over her shoulder, she made eye contact with Mirra, who was sitting in their last remaining turret, pointing the guns at the door. She smiled a little and waved at her. "Everything all right?" Mirra asked over their communications link.

"Everything's fine, I've met with customs and port guys a few times," Spin replied. "I don't think this hangar has been cleaned in a couple decades though."

The grit underfoot was finer than sand, a dark grey, wet grit that seemed to have gotten into every crack and corner of the docking bay they'd agreed to pay for. It was larger than they needed for the Fleet Feather, made for two ships of her class, but the large rectangular hangar was the smallest available. A group of four heavily armoured soldiers approached. The muzzles of the turret guns tracked them as they crossed the large empty space between the hangar doors and Spin, who waited patiently at the bottom of the Fleet Feather's main boarding ramp. One of them opened his helmet visor as he stopped in front of her, and returned the smile she offered him. "Anything you'd like to declare?"

"Just delivering some passengers and visiting an old friend," Spin replied. It was easy to slip into a role she'd played countless times, that of the young, approachable diplomat.

"Are your passengers anyone special? Any celebs?" asked the guard as he looked past Spin up the ship's ramp. The hatch at the top was gilded with an etched pattern of vines and the silver sheen of the metal indicated that it was no basic freighter.

"No one worth noting," Spin said, handing him two one

hundred UCA platinum slips. "No one worth talking about." If the conversion rate between that currency and the local credits was right, that was just over four months of the guard's salary. A bribe large enough to share, and to keep questions to a minimum.

"Understood," the guard said, obviously pleased with her bribe. "Docking fee was four hundred in UCA, or six hundred in unsecured Plat. You have that?"

Spin handed him four thin rectangular chits worth a hundred each, they felt heavy in her hand. It was less than Sun expected the high end accommodations to cost by a quarter. "We don't know how long we'll be here."

"City's kicking up, the Nay assholes are really pushing on everyone's territory and they just brought some firepower in from some salvage run in mad bot territory that's enough to get the corporate bosses thinking about emergency alliances. If your crew does security work, you'll have no trouble finding it here, no matter your specialty. That is, if your local friend doesn't have first rights on hiring you."

"I'm here to see Quino, but we're free agents," Spin said, paying close attention to the guard's reaction.

The colour drained from his face as he stared at her, frozen for a moment. "You have a good stay. Someone will be by once a day for docking fees." He closed his visor and retreated with his comrades close behind.

The small group of seven passengers who weren't staying on as crew began emerging from the ship with Sun in the lead. "Got through the whole speech without too many interruptions," she told Spin. "Most of them are just happy that we found a place that they can book passage from. All but two of them could find a ship going in the right direction within twenty hours. Everyone's got their stack of credits, and no one tried to take extra."

"Della and me set them up with a little food baggie," Nigel added from up the ramp. "Thought they should have something just in case."

"That works," Spin replied. "Who didn't find a ride?"

"Take a guess," Sun said, glancing towards Tamara, the only one that was a true reject from the Countess's court.

Without hesitation, Spin strode towards her. A young man, Herrin, she'd heard Tamara call him, moved to stand between them. "Pardon me," Spin said as she tapped the back of his knee with her foot, putting him off balance before she pushed the side of his face, sending him sprawling across the metal plated deck. Her gloved hand gripped the low collar of Tamara's consuit, and she pulled the startled woman close so they were nose to nose. "You're going to trade my location to the Countess so you can earn your way back into her good graces, and even if you don't, I know you'll sing all about your adventure to your brother."

"No, I'm just going to contact him so one of our ships can get me and Herrin, then I won't tell them anything, I swear on- "

"If you expect me to believe that, then you really think I'm a brainless doll. Tell her that Larken is dead," she said, feeling as though she wanted to take her anger out on the waif right then and there. It was such pure fury; unlike she'd ever known before. "Her pilot murdered him. Her autumn doll set is broken, and she should forget about ever seeing me again. As for you, I should kill you, it's the only thing that really makes sense, flushing you out the airlock like a rim weasel. I'll find out if I'm right, if you tell everyone where I am, and you had better pray I don't have time to find you."

"I suppose you'd kill me then," Tamara said. "Then just kill me now, you'll think I squealed no matter what I do anyway."

"I won't kill you," Spin said, realizing that everyone, not just their departing passengers, was off the ship, witnessing the scene. A realization that something was wrong with the medication that had been keeping her steady since Larken was killed was secondary to the thought that she had to make a point to all the people who she saved, the people who were leaving with her generous assistance. "I will track you down, steal you in the night and disfigure you while we travel to a brand new world. A world that has no use for an ugly, pampered bitch with no practical skills, a world so far from your brother and the rest of your family that they'll never find you. I'll alter your DNA enough so you can't even be found by the best hunters, then drop you off in the middle of the worst slaver territory you could imagine. You'll be lucky if someone kidnaps you so they can sell you for meat." Spin could feel a wash of emotions start crowding her mental state as she pushed the woman away. "Get out of my hangar," she managed before retreating up the ramp with Sun close behind.

"You're not okay," she told Spin as soon as they were out of sight.

"I was afraid of this," Leland said as he walked in behind. "Your body is breaking the therapeutic meds you took to dull things down. It probably sees them as an unwelcome alteration, I'm surprised they worked at all."

Spin couldn't believe she didn't think of that before, and cursed inwardly as she led Sun and Leland into a small machinist room near the rear of the ship and leaned on the counter. "It's not like the meds let me get pissed and that's it. It's all rushing back," she said, squeezing her eyes shut and gripping the counter's edge. Sorrow mixed with fear and hate made her want to curl up in a dark corner and scream until she could calm down and dream of Larken, the one thing she wanted from the universe.

Sun gently stroked her back, concerned. "What's going on? How can I help?"

"The drug she took is almost completely out of her system," Leland said, a tinge of sorrow in his voice, pity in his expression. "Whatever was being suppressed and controlled is coming back all at once. I'm no therapist, but I know you've got to be around people, Spin." He moved to her other side, leaving Sun on her left as she attempted to comfort her. "Look at me," he said clearly and seriously.

Spin obliged and stared into his serious eyes. "What?"

"You lost a lot getting here, but you still have friends, you still have people you can trust. Lean on them, they're grieving too. I wish we had time to rest and take care of ourselves, but we don't. We'll take care of business here, let you rest on the ship whenever we can, but we need you, Spin."

"Compartmentalize," she said, nodding, taking a deep breath. "God, I didn't want to go through this, give me a few minutes, I'll be all right."

"You sure?" Sun asked.

"Yeah, just let me get my head back together."

SIX

The sight of a high class, fast passenger transport in the hangar Dorian tracked his old friends to was enough of a surprise for him to decide on a quiet approach. He was sure that sections of the back of his long coat were even more shredded than usual – the force of his pounding thrusters, even if they were made to operate with as little heat as was possible – would be enough to wear through the material, he was sure. For the first time in months he worried about his appearance.

Would Sun and Nigel notice the artificial sheen to his skin or how tattered his thin armour coveralls and jacket were? He'd been busy becoming a hunter to clear his debt, busy killing for so long that he felt awkward at the prospect of a reunion, even though he'd known Nigel since he was a young teen.

He observed from the broad main doors of the hangar as a short but shapely young woman finished her conversation with the Port Control Officers. Between landing gear, he watched as they beat a hasty retreat at the conclusion of their conversation.

She was not the kind of creature he was used to seeing. He closed the distance between him and the nearest landing strut, using it as a hiding place as he watched her turn towards the boarding ramp. Her long brown hair framed a beautiful face that was soft, but seemed like it was raised in the wild as that visage became harsh, expressive, twisted with a sneer that spat threats that nearly made him shudder. His cybernetic hearing delivered her threat to mutilate and abandon a blonde waif coming off the ship to his ears as clearly as it would be if he was standing next to her.

The fierce, beautiful creature retreated up the ramp as the passengers exited the hangar through the port doors. "What did I just see?" he muttered to himself.

Nigel emerged from the ship and Dorian steeled himself. "New introductions with old friends, time to be social." With as confident a stride as he could muster he approached his long-time friend. "Nigel, what brings you to the most expensive port on this rock?"

Nigel whirled around and peered at him, unsure of who he was at first, but recognition and joy overtook his expression before Dorian was fully out of the shadow of the ship. "I heard you got killed last year!" he erupted, closing the distance and embracing him. "A few upgrades since, wow," he said, holding him at arm's length and tapping on his chest.

"Yeah, some genius rebuilt me, wrapped me up in military skin, doesn't quite have the warmth or soft touch as the real deal," Dorian said.

"But it's you?"

"Yeah, saved the grey matter, bits of organs here and there. It's me."

"Man, it's good to see you," Nigel said. "It's been a bad week."

From the scabs and chemical burns Dorian detected on his friend's skin, he could see he wasn't exaggerating. "Are you and Sun running under a new captain now? You guys leave the Cool Angel?"

"Captain White turned on us, left us behind while the United Core World Authority soldiers took Spin and us into custody. They were after her, but we got sold to a slaver as a bonus. Spin got to us, used this thing to save our butts, but we lost Trevor and," he cleared his throat.

Dorian realized then that there was an important person missing from his sensors. Nigel's uncle Boro would never have left him behind, and Nigel was always in the man's orbit. "Your uncle?"

"Boro caught a round in the head," Nigel said, shaking his head. "Nothing anyone could do."

"Man, I'm sorry," he offered.

"Yeah, moving on though, Spin and Sun are running the show now, gotta keep moving forward like young sharks, things are too dangerous to stay still."

Young sharks, the expression brought memories of growing up with Nigel, Trevor with Boro as the adult who was around whenever he could be. He was the one who first called them that, young sharks, always moving forward, eating everything in whatever parent's kitchen was closest. It's what he called them often enough for it to stick, and Boro was a giant presence in his adolescence since he never had a father figure. His mother was more interested in picking up in port pubs, trying to snag a husband and whatever came with him before it was time for him to depart. She had a pattern that still made him furious from time to time, but Boro was the most solid man he'd had ever known, and he had no interest in his mother. "What's after you? UCA? Slave hunters?"

"Probably, the bounty sheets and wanted notices haven't been updated with our details just yet, so we're walking around free I guess. Maybe for a couple days, anyway."

"Going to see Quino," Dorian realized aloud. He wasn't aware that Sun could know anyone else on the planet. "He's got a head full of power, running big territory now and a whole crew of assassins."

"Assassins?" Leland asked.

"Yeah, it's how he took a lot of the territory down here after the UCA hit our last base. Anyway, who is Spin? She that girl who was down here a minute ago?"

"Oh yeah, you left before she became Cool Angel crew. Her and Boro had a thing starting up right before," Nigel swallowed hard before continuing. "Anyway, turns out she's a rare doll, not a synthetic mind you, but a lab baked human made to order. Got herself away from a Countess, and Captain White traded her for a big payday, but she escaped, sprung us from a messed up situation, and now I guess we're here to trade the ship and either go after White or find a cure for her."

"A cure?"

"Yeah, she's got a life cap, deep genetic one. Maybe has two years left."

The wash of sympathy he felt for her surprised Dorian. He wasn't the same kind of slave she was, didn't have any kind of longevity limitation imposed on him either, but with the push of a button, Quino could end his life. Perhaps he understood her leash because of his own, but for whatever reason he felt he needed to do something. "I'll get you in front of Quino, but he's probably not too happy with me right now. Just so you know. I've been working for him for a while."

Sun emerged from the ship and stopped half way down the ramp, surprised at seeing Dorian. "You're alive! Captain Hoket said you were killed during a raid." She offered him a hug but it became brief and guarded. "Are you all right?" she said, touching his face.

"New and improved," he said. "Nigel says you need to see Quino, I can get you straight there, I can call one of his drivers."

"I was hoping to take a look around the port first," Sun said.

"No, you don't want to do that. This port is fine for parking your ship if you have the plat, but you don't want to go past those doors if you're talking to Quino. Through there," he said, pointing towards the double doors leading to the port control centre. "That's extreme law, keeping this part of the City civilized takes more soldiers with big guns who will slag anyone who looks like they're about to litter. It's war all along their borders, and Quino's one of their biggest problems. No, I can call a ride, they come in here, through those doors like I did," he said, thumbing towards the large hangar doors. "And we get to Red River territory. Not safer, but Quino still talks about you, so I bet you can trade with him at least."

"Good, are you sure our ship will be safe here?"

"Yeah, the war with the gangs is unofficial, so they don't mess with people who bring money into the City Centre, just don't skip out on docking fees, or they'll take it."

"Makes sense," Sun said. "What's the attitude towards escaped slaves here?"

"Slavers get gutted here, slaves get pressed into gangs, rescued by the Central City folk, or strike out on their own if they can. Slavery's dead here, you're good if you have a slave mark on you."

"Good, when do you think we can get going?"

"As soon as you and the captain are ready," Dorian said.

"Oh, Spin's not the Captain, she handed that over to Sun," Nigel explained.

"Well, whenever your people are good to go then."

SEVEN

Della and Mirra were busy in what was left of the hold, taking a final inventory of the clothing, jewellery, and other articles that they wanted to sell when they found someone who would take them. Leland was packing the most useful supplies in the medical bay into smaller kits so they could be divided between crewmembers, what was left would be in small medical crates.

Spin avoided them and anyone else aboard so she could walk the ship and have some quiet. The surge of emotions had come and gone. She was left numb. There would be times of sadness, times when she wanted to tear the universe apart, and everything in between. Knowing what to expect didn't soften the blows, but seeing the ship around her and recalling everything she did while she was under the emotion dulling influence of her medication led her to the conclusion that she didn't want any more. The targeted sedative dulled more than emotional pain. With the effects gone, she was more aware than ever that she had the keys to the Countess' corporate empire. The most updated version of the operational data for all her companies, even the private military arm was right there in her personal computer.

In her drugged haze, she'd only managed to mask its identity, making it look like a standard entertainment network dump, then protect it with a bio-lock, so only she could access it while the data was in the computer grafted to her living skin. The thought of searching through it for an advantage didn't even occur to her until the fog started clearing. The contents of Larken's personal computer filled in whatever information she was missing, and she knew there was personal data there, things she'd want as the sting of loss subsided.

Clearing her head without assistance was already getting easier. Even so, when she arrived in the main seating compartment and her hand came to rest on cushioning that she destroyed days before she was overcome with the need to trade the Fleet Feather for something else, almost anything else. Spin didn't want to spend one more moment on that ship.

Looking through one of the narrow portholes, she could see a battered slider truck drift into the main docking bay doors and most of her crew getting ready to board it. Her feet were pointed at the nearest exit, and before she knew it she was down the port side loading ramp and face to face with something that looked a little like a frazzled android. His synthetic hair only covered half of his scalp, and his skin had a sheen to it that she'd seen before in cheap armoured cyborgs and androids. He wore a tattered armoured long coat that was missing parts of its lower half, burned off, judging from the scorch marks. Beneath he wore the kind of fortified coveralls she'd seen ship service workers use when they had to pass between pressurized and unpressurized environments, but he didn't have a helmet with him.

"Um, hi?" he said, seeming stunned. Those dark eyes revealed vulnerability, uncertainty she'd never seen in an artificial being – something in there was still human.

Spin grinned at him and shook his hand to put him at ease. "Did Quino send you?"

"This is an old friend of ours," Sun said. "Dorian left the Cool Angel for Captain Hoket's crew about a year before you came aboard."

"Good to meet you," he said.

"I'm Spin," she said, unsure of how she should introduce herself to him in terms of her place on the crew. She wasn't the Captain, that was Sun's job, she had more experience running a ship by a decade at least.

"Spin is our sponsor, among other things," Sun explained as though it had always been true.

"Is this yours?" Spin asked, turning towards the slider truck. Its large, round transit emitters were arranged in rough rows beneath the boxy vehicle. They had been upgraded, the largest of the propulsion modules didn't match the normal near ground transport pods. The larger oval discs around the vehicle were from a larger aircraft, there was no doubt the ugly truck was quick and most likely manoeuvrable. "You did the work yourself?"

"Yes, and yes," he replied, extending his hand. "Dorian Kench, gun for Quino at the moment, but ship cracker by trade. You show me a hull, or a security system, and I'll get you in."

"He believes he's one of the best," Nigel said. "He might be right, but don't tell him that," he said to Spin in a mock whisper.

"We could use someone like you where we're going," Spin said, looking at one of the armour plates covering the rear window of the transport.

He shifted awkwardly. "Won't be free for a long time, but you're kind to offer. Those covers rough, I know," he said, patting an armour plate. "I haven't had much time to beautify my truck, I've been pretty busy. I go to some pretty nasty places. Looks rough, I know, but they do the job. The mover pods were installed with more attention to detail."

"I like it," Spin said. "Some of the best things in the universe are formed from necessity, it's the beauty of function."

"I wouldn't go that far," Dorian replied bashfully. "It's home though, and it'll get us to Red River territory. Everyone knows this atmo runner." The rear doors opened to reveal a littered interior. A few seats had been removed to make room for tools and a rudimentary rack that could fold out into a workbench. Old nutrient pack wrappers, a variety of small leisure drug cartons, and other flotsam from the owner's life rattled between the seats lining the sides of the old short atmospheric transport. The ceiling was decorated with video sheets that he'd torn off walls and pillars around the city. Animated advertisements for weapons, virtual experiences ranging from violent to sensual, atmospheric racing cars, and beautiful distant vistas turned the roof into a kaleidoscopic sensation.

"Sorry, didn't expect company," Dorian said.

Spin couldn't help but feel for him as he rushed inside ahead of them and rolled up his bed – a modest pile of blankets and a hard pillow. "I still need a few hours' shuteye sometimes, the old brain likes to wind down and dream every once in a while. I end up taking in the lightshow instead half the time though," he said, offhandedly gesturing towards the roof.

"Why don't you just spray a display surface on?" Nigel asked.

"I put everything I can towards what I owe Quino. Besides, I like the flash of it all. Everything on my roof is trying to get my attention, like this one – it's the third fastest interplanetary runner you can buy, but if you have it you'll only be able to run it at top acceleration for a few hours here and there because you'll break port speed or get yourself splatted because you're going too fast. The advert, the dream is almost better than having one. Or this, she's a real model, people take scans of her and plaster them everywhere to sell their stuff. Here she's selling clothing designs, here a resort, and this is my favourite – she's selling breakfast bars. Did she ever wear any of those clothes for real? Was she at the resort, or did they use her scans to create an image of her running on the beach? Does she even still eat, or did some machine mulch her on Madness Day? I like the way she looks, sure, but I can imagine she's living on a shipment of breakfast bars on an abandoned beach wearing one of those Active Work one pieces. You put all these vids together like a puzzle and you've got a million dreams, and the truth doesn't matter until you buy the shuttle, or meet the girl, you can escape to wherever it takes you."

"I like it," Spin told him, looking at a playback of a walk in a green meadow. Beside it was an advertisement for a comfort sleeper where a caring man and woman were cuddled together by the extra-large swaddling blanket. That wasn't the only example of idyllic beauty set beside images of human comfort. Aside from stolen images of exciting starship adverts and racier women, most of the images reinforced calm, and featured some kind of human contact.

"Are you sure you want to come with us? You can sit this one out if you like, I can handle it," Sun said.

"I need something to take my mind off things. Besides, I'm starting to feel like my old self, I want to be with people I know." A thought struck her as she looked up the empty rows of seats to where Dorian was settling into the pilot's seat. "Where's the Governor? I thought he'd want to be along for this."

"He was the first one off the ship," Nigel said as he made his way between the five rows of seats between him and the front. "Borrowed a hooded robe from our clothing stash and said he was going to meet a contact he found here to see how his world's doing. He actually looked pretty cool for an old guy in that thing. Oh, and he took a stunner with him. Don't think we have to worry much, he said he'd be back within twenty hours." He picked up an empty box with a loud orange and red DICE logo printed on it. "You do a lot of this stuff, man? I watched someone smoke half of one and before he got half way through he was bleeding from his eyes and ears."

"It's different when you're mostly metal and eternaplast, man," Dorian said. "Gotta keep the input high sometimes just to feel like you're part of the world. DICE just keeps me rollin' when I need that big push. No worries." He started the transport and it lurched two meters into the air.

"Is he very different from when you knew him?" Spin asked Sun quietly.

She only nodded slightly. "So, where are we going, Dorian?"

"Sixty Third Street, Red River District, there's a police precinct Quino and his people turned into a night club, that's where he'll be right now. Should be there in a few minutes."

"What have you been up to?" Nigel asked. "The van's new."

"It's an old junker I salvaged right before I got crushed when we were cracking into a ship."

"So that's why you're all rebuilt?"

"All new-to-me parts, except for the bio support package, that's all new gear. I got pinched between the Merciful Dawn, the ship I was crew on, and a bulk transport we were busting into. Sometimes I wish it ended there, but Captain Hoket made a deal with Quino so his people could put my grey matter in this old cyborg, the facial modding so friends and loved ones could recognize me was thrown in for free, I'm still paying for the rest."

"Expensive?"

"Like you couldn't believe, but I'm working it off slowly, collecting some old debts. I just got a little out of my old Captain, actually."

"How is Hoket?" Sun asked.

"Last I saw him he'd laid down his arms and was planting his feet firmly on the ground," Dorian replied.

"What do you mean? Did he retire?" Sun asked, smiling at Dorian's antics.

"You could put it that way. Less I say, the better."

"No worries then," Sun said. "I don't like him much, to be honest," Sun said. "I always thought you should have stayed on with the Cool Angel."

"Looking back on it, I agree, but it doesn't matter now,"

Dorian said. "I'm stuck with Quino until my debt is paid, should take a few years, and in the meantime I'm looking for the Dawn so I have a ship I can crew up once I'm free and clear."

"The Dawn?" Spin asked.

"The Merciful Dawn," Dorian said, speaking the name with praise. "A rescue ship Hoket bought while the crew's remains were still drifting around inside. The ship's artificial intelligence killed 'em all, then the UCA hit it and the whole port it was sitting in with an EMP and moved on. Got her for a few plat and a song. It was my job to clean the Dawn up, get her reprogrammed. She's my dream ship, and I put most of the work in myself. Willy had her last, but he got splattered, so the ship could be drifting in orbit for all I know. Just have to track her down."

"We're looking for Captain White," Spin said. "We owe him."

"Take the Cool Angel for yourself in the process?" Dorian asked. "I know I would."

"How would you do it?"

"While it's on the ground," Dorian said without hesitation. "You find out where White is landing her or docking her, and take advantage of how those hatches open and expose all the perimeter security circuitry. I used to tell him to shut his hatches when he was on the ground, but he likes to fill his ship with all that free portside air."

"He's right," Sun said. "I never thought of it, but there are panels just inside the boarding ramps that aren't hardened to EMP, the ship isn't made for any kind of ground combat or support, it's made to be sealed during a fight."

"Except for her missile bays," Dorian said. "There's nothing to hit with an EMP in there, the compartments are completely hardened."

"Is Quino still at odds with White?" Sun asked.

"I don't know, if I'm being honest."

"Then don't tell him we're going after the Angel, okay?"

"Mum's the word, and if you need any more info about cracking the Cool Angel, just say so. I can even transfer diagrams. I used to wonder how I would crack White's ship during downtime, he and I didn't exactly split on good terms."

"I remember," Sun said. "It's good to see you again."

"No time for the mushy stuff, Lieutenant," Dorian said. "We're here."

"That's Captain now," Nigel corrected.

"Ah, sorry, Captain Ambo," Dorian said with a smirk as the sound of a large clamp latching onto the side of the transport filled the compartment.

Nigel and Dorian left through the back doors first. "The cockpit doors have been stuck since I added the armour," Dorian said. "No regrets though, they've saved my ass a few times this month."

Hot, humid air rushed into the transport when the doors opened. It carried a burnt smell with it, and at a glance she could tell they had landed on a busy rooftop dock. People walked past in great throngs, hawkers shouted at them from the street side, holding what they had on offer over their heads. Two were visible through the doors. "Emergency boosters! Strap them on your boots and forget about 'em until you're falling through the air! Off a high street like this, out of a shuttle door, or maybe you took a wrong turn and you're out the airlock! This is the fix! Stop you long enough to catch another ride, guaranteed!" he shouted, holding small retail boxes over his head with one hand and shining a light on them with the other.

The other hawker she could see held up one garment after another, stretching them out for all to see. "From the United Comfort factory! The bots killed the workers, but left the goods, and I got 'em! Come see the best in survival and comfort gear in the sector at slip one thirteen! We got everything they had, and they ain't makin' no more! Good prices, great- "

Sun stopped Spin from leaving and closed the doors. "Listen, I'll do the talking. Quino was crazy about me when I left, it's one of the reasons I had to go, but I don't know how he feels now, it's been a while since he's tried to get in touch. I doubt he's changed much though, he has a wandering eye, anyone new who is prettier than average can become a major distraction. You're absolutely drop-dead, so I'm wondering if you could, you know?"

"Sure, I'll be a distraction," Spin said. "Who do you want me to pretend to be for this?"

"I've been thinking about that. It has to be close to the truth."

Slipping her finger down the front of her containment suit, Spin instructed it to split open, relaxing its collar and the fit in the front, a relief she found more comfortable than expected. She was used to loose clothing, and the consuit wasn't uncomfortable, the cloth was so smooth that it had a pleasing sheen to it, but she still hadn't grown accustomed to the tight fit, especially from the waist up. Clear of the calming drug's influence, she was more aware of the firmness of the suit, and she enjoyed some relief. Her finger continued down until the front was loosened enough for her tastes, and it stopped before Spin felt too exposed. With a gesture she loosened the shoulders a little, tightened the lower half so it felt like the sort of tights she grew up wearing, then felt more at home in her consuit.

Judging from Sun's amused expression, it looked better as well. "That's more like the Spin I've come to know, but maybe a little more cleavage?" she asked. "We want him as off balance as possible."

Spin obliged, modesty was never precious in her upbringing. "How did he become a gang lord if he's stunned by a little skin?"

"That's not a little skin," Sun chuckled at the adjustment. "He plans further ahead than most, and he uses people, it's one of the reasons why I left. I guess he was successful after the bots went nuts."

She shifted in her jacket and let it hang open. The weight of the armoured garment felt good, and she set the environmental system to match her consuit, which would keep her cool in the heat outside. "All right, then what kind of associate am I? Should I wear this out with confidence, as though I don't care who's looking, or like I'm putting it on display for someone who's looking to spend some money on a flashy digger?"

"Confidence, don't be available to him. The real story, your story is going to make a huge impression on him, he hates slavers, but people – especially women – who are on a mission and don't give him more attention than they have to drive him crazy. So, you'll be Aspen, an escaped slave who is sponsoring me as Captain. It would be too easy for him to find the truth on his own, and I think he'll like having someone who isn't afraid of people like the Countess around, especially if you're walking in like that."

"Advanced diplomacy, get your bargaining opponent off balance, even if it strains self-respect. Not that this gets anywhere near that, I've worn more revealing dancewear and not batted an eye when everyone was staring, to be honest."

"Someday you're going to have to tell me what it was like living with the Countess."

"Someday," Spin said.

"Are you sure you're all right with this? I mean, you're steady enough?"

"I'm good, Captain. Besides, I can't wait to trade the Fleet Feather for almost anything else, especially if it's better armed."

THE HEAT OUTSIDE was mostly thanks to the warm, humid evening, but Spin was certain that the ships coming and going from the old law enforcement docks was a contributing factor. The docks extended out from the round precinct building like spokes on a wheel, with many levels and a high elevation above the other buildings. The people on the broad ramps and narrow streets between dozens of mooring points for small and medium sized ships were all either going somewhere or selling something. The hawkers seemed to be very close to their ships, most of them only had a few samples in hand while their holds were locked tight behind them.

A pair of helmeted spacers in light armour didn't move out of Dorian's way, but he remedied that by effortlessly pressing them to the sides of the ramp. One put his hand on the butt of his pistol, but the other stopped him with an urgent shake of his head. "Is it always this busy?" Spin asked. It wasn't the most urgent question on her mind, but it was a good place to start.

"No, looks like someone major is setting out," Dorian replied. "I've been gone a couple days, had to hunt someone down before meeting Hoket."

"You do a lot of hunting for your boss?"

"It's all I can do to pay off my debt, he hasn't trusted me enough to let me off world yet," Dorian said.

Closer to the main security doors there was a heavy gunship docked, its hull was bristling with paired turret guns. She made eye contact with one of the gunners, who couldn't have been more than eleven years old, and she grinned at her, waggling her turret. Spin winked and waved back at her, hiding the repulsion she had at having someone so young at the controls of a deadly weapon. Even if the child could handle the duties of a gunner, which was doubtful, being behind a weapon at all put her at incredible risk. Gunnery emplacements are always juicy targets.

All the other ships docked around it were being loaded with cargo containers using long arms that reached into a hangar overhead. "Are you sure it's not moving day?" Spin asked.

"Quino has a massive shipping operation. Red River Crew's biggest business is protection, that's why it's so busy here, people can do business here, live under the precinct's shield complex if they're lucky, or just get something across the sector and know it'll get there."

"For a fee," Nigel added. "Probably a big one."

"Sure, but it's not like the Postal Service is still running.

Well, except for a couple couriers, but they're like fucking white knights: few, powerful, and so quick you're not sure you've actually seen one."

"You've met one?"

"Quino says he got a delivery from one shortly after taking over the Red River Crew. I wasn't around then," Dorian replied.

"That's because they're not real, the British Alliance just wants us to believe there's some Postal Corps that's still delivering."

"Why would they lie about that?" Sun asked. "What's the conspiracy this time, Nigel?"

"Just the great big B-A trying to convince everyone that they're better than everyone else, more cultured than us. There's money in that somewhere," Nigel replied.

"There is," Spin said. The Countess was technically attached to the families who brought the British Alliance together, it was one of the critical justifications for her title and role in the old monarchy, even though she knew it was a vestige of another time. The British Alliance did still try to project an image of long standing tradition and culture, that was fact, and they did use it to increase wealth in many ways. "You couldn't image how much their reputation is worth, or what kind of premium businesses used to pay to be associated with them. I don't know if that's true now though."

"No shit," Nigel replied. "But the Postal Corps are gone now, right?"

Spin remembered meeting a tall, blonde man in a navy blue uniform when she was still a girl. She loved the gold epaulets and medals on his jacket and giggled at the toothy grin the stiff-backed man gave her while he waited for a seal bearing member of the Countess' House so he could deliver a hand written letter. His ship was a shining metal wedge, and his uniform was just as spotless as that quick vessel. "I hope they still exist. Something like that can only increase the good in the universe."

"Lady's got a point," Dorian said. "Would be good to run into someone who only has one mission for once, no hidden agendas or ladder climbing ambitions. Hey Ferrah, me and three good friends to see Quino," he told one of four of the heavily armoured guards in front of the main doors leading into the east side of the precinct. "Set us up with an express car, yeah?"

"All right, Dorian, they scan clean enough."

"Just set us up with an express car, I don't want to deal with the gallery crowd."

"Sorry, Zero just finished a fight, Quino is still ringside."

"Fine," he told the guard. "Get ready for a whole variety of drama and grounder trash," Dorian said to Sun and Spin, looking over his shoulder.

The tall armoured doors opened, revealing a second set. They had been adorned with a shield and iconography that probably celebrated the police force that once called the thick precinct building home. The central images had been ground away and replaced with two large R's with a C in the lowest spot using some kind of etching tool. The words 'Red River Crew' were etched alongside the corresponding letters.

They stepped into a boxy transit car with no windows and Dorian punched their destination into the panel. "Trash?" Sun asked.

"Whenever there are enough cyborgs here who will fight,

are desperate enough to fight in the Precinct, Quino plans a few fights. Round robin, fight until you can't, blood sport shit. Lots of money flies around, all the gangs are allowed to put fighters in, but no explosives are allowed. The gangs have to watch from their own places, except each fighter can have three crewmembers. It's always trouble, someone outside the cage always gets killed."

"Then why does he do it?" Nigel asked.

"He loved the cage matches when I knew him," Sun said.

"The money is so huge too," Dorian said. "The Precinct is one of the only places where people know the fighters are going to be scanned, and the fights aren't fixed."

"No way, how can you make sure?" Nigel asked.

"Quino pays to have fixers interrogated and killed. I've seen it done," Dorian said.

"I believe that," Sun said.

The transit car door slid open and the sound of a large crowd, the smells of sweat and smoke overwhelmed Spin. A room large enough for several hundred people had been cleared, and there was a heavily barred cage hanging several meters above the floor. The space was well past comfortable capacity, and the arguing Dorian mentioned was immediately evident. The worst of it surrounded a small group of people in yellow and black near the side of the cage. At least two dozen men and women in prominent colours – some of them obviously cyborgs with visible implants – were having a vicious shouting match. Blood and other fluids dripped from the bottom of the cage as a few men in plastic suits cleared what was left of the most recent losing contestant away.

"You ever fight here?" Nigel asked, wide-eyed.

"Three times," Dorian replied without a hint of pride. "First three things I did for Quino after the rebuild."

"What? You find out you've been rebuilt as a cyborg and the first thing he does is throw you into a cage match?" Sun asked.

While she was asking her question, Spin was watching how the people on the walkway were moving out of Dorian's way as he led them to the middle, to the cage. There was only a little appreciation in how they looked at him, as though they thought he was a serious contender, but most of them regarded him with fear, some with alarm. Whatever Dorian did for Quino, whether it was in or out of the cage, it had earned him a reputation.

"I wasn't exactly cooperative when I was switched on," Dorian said. "It calmed me down."

Spin wondered if it calmed him down, or brought him to heel as she watched Nigel's reaction. Nigel's eyes were darting between the cage in the middle of the space, Dorian, and something up ahead that Spin couldn't see thanks to her height deficiency compared to him. Then she heard it, the sound of one voice cutting through the crowd. "Shut your fucking hole before I fill it with my boot! It wasn't a fair fight, you're right, your guy was overcharged and had an extra set of support servos!" The source of the voice came into view, it was a thick, heavily muscled man with transparent skin across his shoulders and chest. The glint of metal underneath that synthetic flesh revealed that he had most likely replaced most of his bones with a new reinforced metal structure. "The scanners caught it, and Zero over there said he wanted the challenge. I didn't want the fight to go on, but when Zero says he can tear someone up, I believe him, and that's what he did. So you take your scrap metal, pound of flesh, and his brain case home, and explain to your boss why the Raven Sky Crew is banned from the Precinct, got it?" The crowd surrounding him thinned, the group wearing yellow and black were the first to beat a hasty retreat.

"Oh my God, what has he done to himself?" Sun asked quietly, looking at the two-and-a-half-meter tall cyborg who had just dispersed a crowd of twenty with his booming voice.

"It's the Red River Crew way," Dorian said. "They would only allow him to take leadership if he replaced at least half of himself with machines, so he started with his bones to prove himself even more."

Quino took a long drink from an amber bottle marked with a large M then put it down on the edge of a squared off set of box seats. "Dorian, good to see you made it back, I was about to push your button."

"Got a little side tracked, and found some friends," Dorian explained as he led Nigel, Sun and Spin to Quino's side.

"If you didn't end Chuck before you murdered Hoket, I'd care a lot more, but you're not in trouble. Leaving Chuck where you did put the scare in those gutter rats." Until Spin got close enough to see differently, she thought Quino was wearing a jacket that was transparent in the shoulders and open across the chest, but she was mistaken. His skin was pierced with loops along his back and sides, and grey cloth hung from them, draping down to the floor. She could see a shimmer above them, like there was some kind of energy all around him, and she suspected they were the source.

"Holy shit, is that Sun?" he said, a giant smile spreading across his human looking face.

"Good to see you again, Quino," Sun said, offering him a hug as though he hadn't changed at all since she'd last seen him.

A slight puff of air and the disappearance of the shimmer surrounding Quino told her that his personal shield had been lowered. He was very gentle with an embrace that was a little too long. "Man, it is good to see you. Where's White?"

"You didn't hear?" Sun asked, taking a pair of steps back. The slight aura of energy around Quino returned. "He tried to sell us to slavers through the UCA."

Quino's smile disappeared. "That piece of shit," he muttered. "Don't tell me Boro and his guys stayed after that."

"Boro was sold too, got killed escaping. I don't know about the rest of his guys."

"Nigel?" Quino asked, turning to him. "You filled out, boy. I didn't recognize you. Sorry about Boro, he was one of the best. Not just machinists, mechanics, but people. C'mon, let's get to the office, I don't want to give these Crew and Clan shitheads something to gossip about." He led them part way around the cage, where Zero was having a woman with spikes jutting from her head in rows attend to his damaged mechanical arm. A hatch opened in the floor, and they followed Quino and two soldiers in heavy red powered armour down a set of stairs.

The office below was filled with holographic projections of different arenas, most of them were empty. One of the largest projections featured a larger arena with sun baked sand and a muscular man in a gilded loin cloth getting ready to announce new contestants. "The show doesn't stop, not really, so the betting never stops. Zero is getting fixed up and will be fighting in the Gyro tomorrow." He offhandedly pointed to an arena cage that was slowly spinning and tilting.

"Against the Noran?" Dorian asked.

"Against Noran."

"He's going to get killed. He's not allowed to upgrade anymore and his balance is shit."

"He doesn't think so, and his career should have ended a dozen fights ago," Quino said. "So I let him fight. I'm betting against him, yeah, but he'll probably win just to stick it to me. You interested in vying for champion of the Precinct when he goes down?"

"No, Sir," Dorian said.

"You know, I didn't have a dick installed when you were put back together, but I don't remember having a pussy put in either," Quino sneered. "Go see Xem, she's got someone for you to track down."

"All right," Dorian said. "Good seeing you again, and good meeting you, Spin. Here's my ident, just in case you come this way."

"Don't worry, I'll give them your ident, fuck off," Quino said. Dorian retreated down the hallway in one direction as Quino led them in the other direction. "Something's wrong with that kid. He won't fight in the arena anymore, but he'll kill anyone I point him to outside the cage. With his mods, he could take Zero out, maybe, definitely most of the ladder under him, but that wouldn't clear his debt. Close, but not quite."

"How much does he owe?" Nigel asked.

"Oh, that's right, he's your cousin, right?" Quino asked.

"Old friend."

"Right, grew up together. I remember him telling me. I'm sure it's more than you've got, if that kind of platinum landed on this world, I'd know about it." They came to a broad set of double doors and entered a room wallpapered with displays of the megacity. They were enhanced by holograms that focused on different major events. A violent conflict between people on two skyscrapers was the focus of the right side of the room, and the arrival of a scarab-like ship atop the Precinct was the focus on the right. Before Spin could see more, Quino dismissed the holograms with a gesture. He sat in a chair that rapidly rose from the floor. It was transparent plastic on the outside, but was filled by water jets that caused the surface to ripple and push against whoever sat down. A long seat across from him did the same, and the trio sat down. "So you've come hat in hand to me now that I'm top dog of the Red River Crew."

"No, actually," Sun said. "We've got financing, that's not the problem. What we don't have is a fighting ship, but we have one we could trade for it."

"I guess that's where the one you haven't introduced me to comes in," Quino said, leaning towards Spin. "Spin. Who is Spin?"

"Escaped slave," she replied as she ignored his inspecting eyes. One of those wasn't human anymore. He was taking a scan. "Kidnapper, thief, and the financial backbone."

Quino sat back, his seat shifting with his weight slightly. He didn't speak, but looked the three of them over as if taking them seriously for the first time. Spin knew this game. If she filled the silence with more information, or some pointless quip, he would win. If he was a master negotiator, he was trying to keep them off balance, but it was more likely that he had some kind of connection to the solar system's Internet. He was looking them up. Looking her up. She was about to find out if word of their wanted status had arrived.

"You're a doll," he said as though turning the information over in his head. "But who did you escape from? You're rare, everything about you is behind an old Geist paywall, so even they thought someone might try to steal you if they knew what you looked like."

"You'll hear about it soon enough, but that doesn't matter," she looked to Sun, who nodded.

"We have this high speed luxury transport to trade, I thought you might be interested," Sun said, projecting a hologram of the Fleet Feather into the middle of the room.

Quino whistled his appreciation. "Damn, I haven't seen one of those in years. I'll give you three hundred million plat right now for her, a little high, considering the damage, but I know having a sky chariot like that will make an impression. Especially if I install a new shield."

"We need to trade for a better armed ship," Sun said. "We're going to need firepower where we're going."

"Sorry, can't help you. All the Crews are fighting the Nays, and when we're done taking those anarchists out, we'll go right back to fighting each other full time. This is the wrong system to find an armed ship in. Now, if you have a couple months to spare, I could convert something for you. Something bigger, more cargo space, maybe almost as fast with custom guns like you've never seen," Quino said.

"You don't have anything ready you could trade to us? I mean, I could pick up a ship with racks and class five firepower in Owano for two-twenty-five, and that's with thrusters to match."

"That's Owano, not here. I've got people off world raiding ports that've been taken over by AI's and hitting dead worlds, looking for anything that has a gun and will turn on just to keep pace with the Nays so I can hold this place. Why don't you and miss money here go hit Lokun or Siritis, they've got more ships than they can handle and only take plat."

"That's in the wrong direction," Nigel said.

Quino laughed and pointed at Spin. "You're hers," he said. "You were that doll that got away from the Countess on Bad Bot day! No wonder White turned you over, you were probably his retirement plan once he managed to get the UCA to cough up their private most wanted list."

"Private list?" Spin asked.

"Yeah, it's the special most wanted. The ones the ultra-rich and super connected pay them directly to retrieve. If everyone knew it was real, they wouldn't exactly look like the good guys to the liberation folks, people like us. People who hate slavery. Makes them look like a bunch of thug bounty hunters."

"You seem to have quite a few slaves yourself," Spin said.

"People owe me money and can't pay," Quino said. "They do the jobs I think they can take, the ones that will get them out from under debt as fast as they can. For your buddy, that's assassination for hire. He's the Red Crew murder man."

"Slaver," Spin said quietly. Her temper was getting the better of her.

"Not for a fucking minute! I could let the kid sweep floors and clean toilets, but he'd be here for a hundred fifty years!" Quino shouted, his voice so loud that it made her ears ring. He shifted and settled in his seat then shook his head. "This one knows how to get under people's skin," he laughed. "Draws you in with honey and hyacinth and slips the blade right in. You tell her that guilt grinds me? Or did she figure that out on her own?"

"I barely had time to tell her anything," Sun said.

"What's your bond to her? She paying you?" Quino asked.

"She saved me, and she's my friend."

"Well, it's still no on the ship, but I'll have my people repair your ship. Cost, no labour. It'll be done in three days."

"You haven't seen the damage," Nigel said.

"I have," Quino said, pointing to his temple. "Little brain bud in here's got me connected to all the major networks. Probably cost you thirty-five thousand in parts if you want some armour with your plating, twenty if you have stamped plat."

"Molecularly stamped and certified United Core World Authority platinum?" Spin asked. "I'll give you twelve thousand."

"Eighteen," Quino said. "And I'm eating a little of that cost."

"A treasury was just hit; value will be going up. You'll make a profit at fifteen, but you're letting us down, so that drops to fourteen."

"Prettiest hard-nosed negotiator I've ever seen," Quino said. "I'll do it for fourteen, and I'll make sure they don't cut corners. No furnishings or decorations though."

"Deal," Spin said. "And if you get word of an armed ship with a good flank speed, you tell us first."

"No promises," Quino said. "But you can steal whatever you want from any other Crew in the system. You won't get my blessing, but I'll look the other way – even if I have an alliance with whoever you hit."

"We've got some work to do if repairs are going to happen," Sun said, standing. Spin and Nigel followed her lead.

"You could stick around," he said to Sun. "All of you if you want, next fight starts soon, should last a while too."

Nigel flashed a pleading look at Sun, who shook her head. "It was good seeing you again, Quino. We'll be ready for your guys in a few hours."

Quino nodded and gestured towards his guards, who silently led them out of the Precinct to a waiting shuttle.

EIGHT

Dorian shuddered as Quino entered the room behind him. He'd seen the exchange, Xem sat him down and told him to watch before slinking from the concrete and steel space. "That Spin is a real spiked peach," Quino said. "She's going to fit right into a few special sims I've been looking for new flesh for. You were watching?"

"Yes, you gave them a really good deal on repairs," Dorian said. It was a quarter the cost of parts in the end, better than anyone deserved, unless they were trading more than they thought.

"After the last round of rebuilds, I'm up to my ears in scrap, the parts are nothing. Besides, with what I know now I'm in profit within the week. The Cool Angel is without her most experienced lieutenant, and I have a hunter who knows that ship in and out."

"I'm sure they've changed the codes since I left." He had no love for Captain White, but he was sure there were still people he liked in his crew. He didn't want to be the one to wrest the prized ship from them. He didn't like what that might take.

"White fucked you over for thousands, left you in an unfriendly port when you stood up to him. That's enough for a death mark, let alone his removal as Captain. I haven't seen eye to eye with the man for years, so I don't give a shit if you have to kill him, but I want that ship. I'll even make you a deal," Quino leaned in close, his mechanical eye glinting green. "You bring me the Cool Angel with all its major systems functioning and the value of everything inside gets deducted from your debt to me. There's got to be a haul on that ship, otherwise White wouldn't be in Naro Port, finishing a refit. That's a day from here."

"In a fast ship," Dorian said, his heart sinking.

"Like the Fleet Feather. This is it, boy, your chance to get off world, to finish paying me off this week."

"There won't be enough aboard that ship to pay you off," Dorian said. "Even if White did just get paid for turning Spin in."

"Then I'll make the deal even sweeter. You get five thousand for every crewmember you kill to get the Cool Angel in my docks. I don't care if they're Cool Angel crew, or Fleet Feather crew, or if you leave one crew completely alive. Just get that ship in my docks."

"Give me fifty thousand if I kill Captain White," Dorian pressed.

"He had a talent for pissing me off, so I'll give you thirty-five. You get nothing for killing Spin and Sun though. Knowing that kind of beauty is in the universe makes me smile, even if they'll hate me when you're done."

"Done. What do I tell them? How do I get them to take me there?"

"Tell them you know where Captain White is, and how to get onto his ship. The rest you'll have to improvise, but I've seen you kill, boy. Improvising is one of your strong suits. You've got seven days, then that little cap in your chest goes off."

Dorian's hand touched his breastbone – now a metal plate that held the cage protecting his artificial organ package – without realizing it until he was rubbing the spot. That would be the end of him, no more Dorian, no more high times, no more adventures between the stars. The risk would be worth it. Freedom from his contract, no more killing unless he decided someone should be done in. He could find the Dawn, crew her up and point her wherever he wanted. "Seven days, aye."

NINE

The shuttle didn't drop them off at the ship, but one of the lower levels beneath the main port levels. The open air walkways should have provided a cooler experience, but the rising sun only turned the heat up, and the humidity wasn't clearing. Spin's jacket and suit worked together to keep her cool, but Nigel had taken a lesser garment that protected from the extreme cold of space, but didn't react to more subtle changes in temperature. Within minutes, he'd pulled the upper half of his loose jumpsuit down to his waist and stretched out his long arms. "It's not much better, but at least I can feel that breeze," he said.

The crowd of thousands made their way along a walkway that wove in and out of the building, suspended hundreds of meters over a ramshackle slum. Everyone had somewhere to go, and security kept people moving along the walkways, and even though the trio were focused on not getting separated as they made their way, Spin could tell something was wrong when she looked at Sun. "What's going on?"

"I thought you were going to let me do the talking?"

"I'm sorry, it seemed like he was more interested in talking with me instead," Spin replied.

"You almost set him off. That wasn't the Quino I knew from years ago, he's changed, he's not just ambitious anymore, he's dangerous."

"I'm sorry, did you want to go back and flirt with him for a while? That was your plan going in, right?" Spin asked, regretting the comment only a little.

"Maybe, but as soon as I saw how he'd changed, that went out of the window, I had a new plan, but you were in negotiations with him before I had a chance to lay it out for him."

"What was it?" Spin asked as they made their way around a tall hover cart with a closed cargo cab.

"You want to know now? There's not much point."

"I really do, because he wasn't interested in what we were there for. Trades were off the table."

"Sure, but that doesn't mean he couldn't lead us to a loose port where we could steal something right off the ground. I didn't even get a chance to ask him what happened at his last base, or try to sell the parts we got there."

"Leave some other crew without their ship? I'm not a fan of screwing some struggling band of people we don't know. As for the parts, I don't think we'll have a problem hocking them. You're right though, he was willing to deal, we got our repairs for practically nothing."

"That's if the craftsmanship is any good," Nigel said.

"Okay, but you get why I'm pissed, right?" Sun said, ignoring Nigel's comment.

"I do, I made you Captain because of your experience," Spin replied, conceding so she could restore the peace, not because she entirely agreed with her.

"We should still be there, talking things over and gathering information. We don't even know who the Nays are, and they seem to be the big black cloud hovering over this whole place. There's so much we have to learn about this entire corridor of ports, we've only been through maybe a dozen out of the hundreds that occupy this part of the sector."

"You're right, I cut that shorter than it should have been," Spin said, feigning regret.

"I'm glad you see that. If you're going to make me Captain for this trip, you're going to have to trust me. I'm going to make sure we get everything we can out of every situation without getting our skin singed."

"I know, I will, you do have more experience," Spin said. That was completely true. There was a lot she knew about the universe that came with her intensive education, but running a starship crew and their crew wasn't exactly in the curriculum. "Until you need me to be in the conversation, I'll watch and learn. These crime lords and port bosses aren't anything like the people I knew growing up."

"Exactly, thank you, Aspen," Sun said. "I mean, Spin, sorry."

"It's okay, I'm sorry I took you off track with Quino."

"Now that you two have straightened out the command structure," Nigel said as they picked their way through a broken line of cargo carts and slowly moving pedestrians. "I was wondering, what's up with the name change?"

"It felt right," Spin said. "And it goes with tradition from a couple centuries ago when slavery was first abolished in the British Alliance Territories. Millions of slaves who were named by their masters when they were born took a new name to celebrate their freedom."

"Spin, I like it," a woman whispered near her ear as she passed. She had a stunning, playful smile, blue eyes and white hair. "I took Omira as my name. Take cover if you love your life," she said with a wink before dropping a heavy helmet on her head. The entire surface of her plated armour began animating in a riot of gold and white light as she rocketed upward. Luminous wings spread from her armour – a holographic illusion, but spectacular nonetheless. She hovered overhead for a moment, pressing a control on the arm of her light power suit. "We, the citizens of this galaxy have seen your plans for the new order, the same as the old order, and say nay!" her distorted voice cried through a micro-amplifier.

The sides of the cargo carts they had been passing fell away to reveal over twenty fighters in various types of armour. They immediately opened fire on the security guards as they took to the sky. Some of them had holoprojection built in, giving them multi-coloured angel or butterfly wings. Watching them move through the sky was stunning, a riot of colour and fire as they quickly bested the security who watched the moving throng of people from the sides of the walkways.

"Spin! Down!" Sun said as she dragged her to the deck.

"They're after an inner access point," Nigel pointed out. Following the direction his finger indicated revealed three Nays who fired high explosive rounds at the side of the building above. After four explosive impacts most of them rushed inside.

"It's the Nova Bank vault," one of the ducking pedestrians said. "Guess it's going to be a busy day at work."

"This is a bank hit?" Sun asked.

Before anyone could answer her question, a pair of fighters swept down and hovered in front of the rough opening in the side of the building, blasting the crowd below with hot air. A thickly furred young man with a long snout teetered on the edge of the walkway, and Spin rushed towards him without hesitation.

Buffeted by the air pressing down thanks to the fighters overhead, she almost made it to him in time. Her fingers touched his furry chest as he topped over the edge. Her eyes locked with his terrified visage for only an instant before she remembered that there was an emergency grappling line built into the sleeve of her jacket, and she fired at him. To her surprise, it wrapped around his chest, and Nigel's arms wrapped tightly around her middle. The line went taught, and she thought the three of them were about to go over for a moment, then Nigel sat down abruptly, anchoring them more than enough with his large feet planted on the edge of the railing. "Gotcha!" he declared.

Spin watched as the well furred pedestrian pendulum-swung back towards the broad walkway beneath them and climbed up over the railing so he was safely standing below. He waved up with a toothy smile that was exaggerated by his long snout. Explosions above, and the sounds of the crowd nearly panicking all around drew her attention back to the scene of the robbery.

The starfighters opened fire on something within, and to Spin's surprise, Omira emerged, an energy shield held across one arm protecting her from the fighter's energy blasts, and a canister of some kind in the other. Spin watched in wonder as the woman in angel armour planted her feet firmly on the canopy of the fighter and affixed the canister onto the side of the craft with a thud. One of her companions did the same to the other fighter, and then it became evident that the canisters were actually portable thrusters. As they fired, the fighters were thrown off balance, and the pilots struggled with the controls as they spun through the shield that protected the building.

Omira and her comrades timed their escape so they could follow the fighters through the shield, then disappear into dangerous gangster territory. "Did you see that?" Sun asked. "One of them was carrying a data node that must have had room for thousands of petabytes of data, and enough processing power to run half a dozen ships."

"Can't stop 'em," Spin heard someone in the crowd say. "They kill our security, hack into everything."

"Who are they?" Spin asked the muttering business man as he got to his feet, straightening his beige jacket.

"You don't know?" he asked incredulously. "Not from here, right? You should keep going then. At least worlds that allow slavery can keep a human bank secure."

"Thank you!" an excited voice said from behind her. The caramel coloured fur of the young man she'd saved was all around her then, as he pulled her to her feet and briefly embraced her. "Thank you both!" he said as he pulled Nigel to his feet and hugged him as well. "I would have been one with the ground if it weren't for you, and I'm not even supposed to be working today."

"You're welcome," Spin said. "I couldn't stand to see you go overboard."

"My names Gauruii," he said in a thick, growling accent that was more rolling than menacing. "But all my human friends call me Gary. I was on my way in to use my upper lift key."

"Good to meet you, Gary," Spin said, beaming a smile at him. "What do you do here?"

"I can't say, it's nothing criminal, just private," he replied quietly. "Are you headed up? I can get you into the express lift, the least I could do."

"We are," Spin replied. "Our shuttle ride wasn't interested in dropping us off at our doorstep. We're in the second docking tier."

"I can get you right there, we just have to get inside." He noticed Sun then and fixed her with an admiring gaze.

"I'm Sun, their Captain," she said to him.

He took her hand gently and momentarily lowered his nose to it. "You have beautiful black hair. It's rare amongst my people."

"Nafalli? Somewhere past Joorinan?" Sun asked.

"How did you know? You must be a career traveller," Gary said as he began to slowly lead them towards the large double doors leading into the building. They were stuck open, thanks to a little damage to the hinges.

"I've been port hopping for longer than I'd like to say," Sun said. "Are you sure you won't get into trouble for letting us use your lift pass?"

"As long as I'm with you, and you get out first. I'm headed to the administration level, so your tier is on the way. I'm interested to know, have you ever been through Nurinan?"

"I was thinking of visiting again sometime soon," Sun replied. "I can't stop thinking about a spa I spent the weekend at that was built way up in an ancient tree with a spring running through it. They said the sap and the water made a natural healing pool, and I'll never forget it."

"I've only heard of Illerr Awo, but I've never been. Did the pool live up to expectations?" Gary asked with interest.

"Do I look forty-nine?" Sun asked. Seeing that the question was about to lead to at least one more question, she added; "It works, trust me, I don't look a day over twenty-eight."

"Oh, that is quite something, so many years of wrinkle-sagging, you humans age terribly," Gary said.

The conversation continued the whole time they made their way to the priority lifts, and as they were elevated to their docking space. Spin didn't pay much attention; she was still thinking of the angel that fought in the golden sunlight of dawn. There was something about Omira that was familiar, especially when she smiled.

TEN

The cargo bay was a mess. Anything that wasn't secured in the small storage area for tools and repair supplies was tossed like a mechanical salad. She had time before any of the non-human world based banks would get back to her about where her money could be picked up, and how much was left. Idle hands gave her too much time to think, too much time to remember Larken, Trevor, and Boro, who seemed to come up much more than she expected. He was one of those crewmembers who quietly kept the peace and seemed connected to everyone.

Finally, she found a hand cutter that might help with cleaning up the damage to the rear of the ship. Spin turned and was about to announce her small victory to Nigel when she bumped into Dorian as he stepped into the hatchway.

"I couldn't let them do it."

"You scared the crap outta me," Spin said. "I didn't even know you were here."

"I didn't exactly knock. I thought I should talk to you first, I can see who really makes the decisions."

"About?"

"I couldn't let them watch you leave without telling you that we can lead you right to a ship, and I can help you take it. The Cool Angel is less than a day away."

"What?"

"I can help you get the Cool Angel, you have to do something for me first," Dorian said. He turned around and pointed awkwardly at a spot between his shoulders. "My tracker is right here, you'll get into trouble with Quino, but if you remove it for me, I'll join your crew, crack ships for you, whatever you need."

"Sun might take some convincing, she still thinks Quino could be a valuable friend."

"You wouldn't be able to stay for repairs either. I came to you because I think you can convince Sun, otherwise I would have snuck up on Nigel."

"I can, I know she wants payback on Captain White. She's not saying it, but I can see her jaw lock every time someone mentions his name."

Spin caught a glimpse of Sun as she walked past the doorway then took two steps back to look inside the compartment. "Dorian? What's going on?"

"I need your help, and to warn you. Quino isn't good at hiding his friends, that's why I took you to him in my old beater. I didn't want any of the crews who watch the sky above the Precinct to see your ship coming and going. It didn't work, you're in as much danger as any of the Red River Crew's friends now. When his repair people show up, the other crews will know you're with him for sure, and I know you're really not."

"Can we trust his repair crews?" Sun asked.

Dorian hesitated, then shook his head. "I need you to help me too, I have to get away from him, from this world."

"You didn't answer her question," Spin said.

"No, no you can't. If the ass end of this ship wasn't half hanging open, I'd say take off, get going, but I don't know, maybe you could use a patch up, even the kind you have to watch."

"We can get around that," Sun said. She looked him up and down, and Spin knew why. Even through all those cybernetics, Dorian was looking increasingly anxious. "Red River Crew is in trouble?"

"The Nays just landed a big victory thanks to an outside group they hired, Omira's people, the Empress crew. The fighting is about to get so bad, I don't want to be here. Quino is going to put me on the front line, and I'm sick of killing. I thought I'd come to you and trade the Cool Angel's location for my freedom. Maybe you could dig this tracker and the explosive with it out of my back at the same time."

"You know where it is?" Sun asked, surprised.

"Quino tracks it, he hates Captain White, so the location was sitting right there in the computer system, only an hour ago a refitting crew was starting finishing work on the Cool Angel, less than a day away." He projected an image of the Cool Angel, its sleek, elongated oval body docked in a service bay. A few armour panels had been removed to provide access to the shield systems. The next image featured Captain White walking between the main thrusters. "See? He's replaced two of his burst thrusters with barrier models. He just landed a major payday for that kind of work."

"I wonder if the rest of the crew knows he sold us out?" Sun asked.

"I don't know, but it doesn't look like he'll be there for too much longer, maybe three days?"

"Unless he's getting that whirlpool he always wanted." Sun thought a moment, staring at the image of Captain White.

It felt like there was a fiery ball in Spin's belly, all the anger she'd been collecting threatened to burn her from the inside out, and she was having trouble keeping it to herself. "I don't think he'd be expecting us, and I could change our transponder on our way."

"You want revenge," Sun said. "So do I, but we have to be smart about this."

"I'll help, I owe him," Dorian said.

"You'll be joining this crew. You'll have to follow orders."

"Aye-aye!" Dorian said, snapping to attention. "Have to get the tracker out of my back first, it'll blow if I go too far."

"We might be able to do that," Sun said. "Let our med-tech take a look."

"Is the Governor back?" Spin asked.

"He's not far, just a few levels down talking to a few people from Midtown. He's been checking in like a good diplomat. I'll tell him to wrap things up."

"I'LL GO SEE how Nigel's doing with his assessment of the damage." She found him only a few steps away, on the other side of the bulkhead eavesdropping. As soon as he noticed her, Nigel hurriedly led her off the ship to the doors leading deeper into the station. "What's going on?"

"He's not the same," Nigel said. "Okay, okay, I know, that's the most obvious thing I could say, but I mean there was something you could trust about Dorian before. He would overreact sometimes, but he was a good guy, and people would usually see that within minutes. Now, there's something way off, not just weird, but enough so I don't really know if that's still him in there. It's like someone made a doll of my friend – oh God, bad choice of words, I'm so sorry."

"That's all right," Spin said. "Finish your thought."

"I look at him, and either there's something really broken, or something missing completely. Like they forgot to install a soul or something. God, that sounds stupid. I just can't put my finger on it, but I don't trust him."

"What do you think about following him to the Cool Angel?" Spin asked.

"If he knows where it is, then yeah, we've gotta make sure the rest of White's crew knows what he did to us at least. That shit can't stand, but we've gotta go in with our eyes open."

"What do you think of taking the Cool Angel for ourselves? Could Sun get enough votes from the crew to take command?"

"Almost everyone likes Sun, she was a Lieutenant on that ship for a long time, so she's got a shot, but if we're going to use the Angel to go after your cure, then we'll have to find a way to make money on the way, or sell the idea of stealing tech from Geist to the crew. Otherwise, there's no way Sun will get voted up as the captain. That is if we can kill White. He's got people aboard who have been backing him for years."

"You have no problem killing your old captain?"

"I hope I don't have to do it, but I don't feel too bad about him getting fragged, no. Boro and Trevor would be alive if it weren't for him. He's got to go, dead or marooned is cool with me."

"All right," Spin said. "We're only getting the location of –" her comm beeped. "– the Cool Angel if we take Dorian with us."

"All right, but we have to keep an eye on him, and he can't be the one calling the shots when we try to take the ship."

Spin's comm beeped again and she tapped her cheek to indicate that she had a call. "I agree. One sec, just finishing something up," she said to the caller.

"It's Mitch," said the Governor's voice through her subdermal comm. "There's someone who wants to meet you, and I think you should take her up on it. She's in the Three River Palace, level fifty-six. Just you, I can stick around if you'd like me to facilitate."

Spin thought for a moment. Only stunners were allowed within the Midtown Port Building, so the danger was limited. Her suit and jacket made her mostly immune to stuns, so the danger was limited. "I'll be there in a few minutes." She ended the call and regarded Nigel. "How's the ship?"

"I can get a lot of the damaged surround on the starboard turret cleared so I can finish repairs on it from the inside, but the breaches aft will need a lot of time and material. If we're not sticking around so Quino's guys can do the work, then it's going to have to stay the way it is."

"I'm afraid we'll have to get the work done somewhere else, unless we end up on another ship somehow."

"Yeah, I was wondering about that," Nigel said. "What if we don't get the Angel? Do we go port hopping until we find someone who will trade this for something that can hold its own in a fight?"

A thought occurred to Spin then. All the details about the Countess' private military forces were sitting in the biological data storage on her arm. Approaching any of it was risky, but it could give them options. "I have a contingency. We should try to find a port where ships hit by the UCA's attacks are being reconditioned, but if that doesn't work out this week, we'll move on to another plan."

"You actually have another plan? Like not taking the Angel, not trading this luxury heap, but something else completely?" Nigel was so surprised that Spin could only laugh.

She handed him her sidearm, it was too high powered to make it through the building's interior security scanners and smiled at him. "I'll share when there's time, don't worry, and don't fall in love with this ship. We'll be aboard something we can take into a fight before you have a chance to get this thing tuned."

"Thank God," he said. "Where are you going?"

"To pick up the Governor," Spin replied as she walked through the security door leading into the building.

ELEVEN

Aldo's job as a guard had saved him from financial ruin, the Partisan War, the day the artificial intelligences went mad, and from an uncertain future in one of the thousands of wastelands that those chaotic events left behind. He hadn't seen perimeter duty for over five years, and being close to old royal family members, being one of the few that they fully trusted afforded him the best placement and many privileges. For most of his career, he enjoyed the position, and his partner, Corrine, still did.

As a pair they were as vigilant as ever, as helpful to the people they were charged with protecting as ever, but Aldo couldn't shake a rising unease at what he was doing and a distaste for who he had been tasked with guarding. Master Kort was cruel by default to everyone he saw as his inferior except for the guards and his crewmembers. That was his whole name, Kort, like some media star, he'd dropped the other half of his name. He was the Countess' consort, and the only one, but he had almost as much power as a husband.

When Kort's people called on Aldo and Corrine specifically days before, he was sure they were about to be reprimanded for giving young Aspen food before her escape. It was only a meal bar, but it was a violation of instructions nonetheless. He was surprised when they were reassigned as Kort's personal guards. His previous guards were promoted, leaving a void that had to be filled. The pay raise was incredibly high, and the rise in position would eventually offer new opportunities.

The down sides were just as clear. They would rarely have time to spend any of that money, and Kort rarely required guarding, so the post promised to test their patience. One thing Aldo didn't think about was all the meetings and inner circle workings they'd witness.

It was just such a meeting that Aldo and Corrine were tasked to escort Kort to in the early evening. In a part of the palace they'd never seen before was a suspension pool filled with viscus gel, and the Countess stretched her long limbs out in the middle of it. It was easy for Aldo to avert his eyes the moment they entered the lushly furnished room. Kort settled on a settee that was hand crafted with actual wood and real cotton fabrics. Large statues of birds overlooked the Countess' large pool, their shadows seemed otherworldly in the dim artificial light. Through a giant circular skylight the night sky did what it always managed to do for Aldo – put on a show of natural light and colour he had difficulty looking away from.

"Kort, it took you long enough."

"I responded as soon as I received your summons," Kort

said. "I was with my Lieutenants, planning the first stage of our journey to Geist."

"That will be on hold. Instead, I want you to supervise the installation of trackers in all my slaves. After some thought I've come to realize that times have changed, and I will be taking away many of their privileges, since they don't seem to be enough to inspire gratitude in my workforce."

"The escape attempts will pass with time, but I agree. It's time to begin tracking all our assets. I'll have Captain Tindol attend to it immediately."

"No, you will be there to see every slave have their band installed. When the banding is complete, you will assemble the slaves in groups and demonstrate what happens when an escape attempt is made. You will do this for me because you are the cause of all this trouble. Your lecherous advance pushed my poor Autumn children away, I've seen the footage."

"I was only showing Aspen her place, but I will do as you command."

"Am I not a delight to look upon?" the Countess asked, standing from the pool slowly. Her body was so elongated and thin in feature that she barely looked human at all. How she could stand up straight, Aldo didn't know or want to know, but her long face and head seemed too large for her neck, her waist was unnaturally thin, and her skin was as pale as maggots.

"Your beauty is unparalleled in the universe," Kort said as he stood and kissed her outstretched hand. "I'd love nothing more than to join you."

The Countess smiled coyly. "If only there was time, my consort. No, you will begin banding the slaves tomorrow, to be finished in two days, and while that is underway you will personally begin pursuing Aspen and Larken. My usual methods have turned up nothing, the pair of them are too well educated to be trapped by these half rate slave hunters or our basic security. They've caused significant damage, in fact." The Countess settled back into the thick bath with the assistance of a pair of slaves.

"The nutrient farm, I heard. They also made off with almost all of the slaves who were captured with Aspen."

"Has the one we revived revealed anything about where they could be headed?"

"No, Boro Lozel doesn't know anything, but he has revealed a list of ports the Cool Angel regularly visits. This should take weeks to resolve if the UCA are looking."

"I have made sure that only our internal security is aware that Larken and Aspen have escaped. Not even your fleet has been notified, nor will they be."

"What? Why?" Kort asked.

"This is family business, there is no reason to get outside parties involved."

"This is no time to let your pride interfere with business. Last time Aspen escaped, she had chaos as her cover, but now she has money thanks to that kidnapping fiasco, and she has Larken. As a pair they can achieve anything."

"This is a private matter, they are wayward children who don't know what they're doing, where they're going."

"They're intelligent, well educated fabricants who have broken their mental conditioning. They have a head start and enough platinum to get them quick transport along with a fast ship. You underestimate them, you always have."

"Nevertheless, you will find them. No more great houses

and no branches of law enforcement have to know they've escaped again. They will be returned to me alive. We have reprogrammed them both before, it will be done again."

"I will find them for you, Countess. My fleet is already prepared for the Geist expedition, I can deploy ships to search within the hour," Kort said, beginning to bow.

"No! You will find them!" the Countess burst. "Choose an inconspicuous ship with whatever crew you deem necessary and make chase. Bring them back to me, rescue my children and I'll pay you in an act of equal devotion."

"Marriage?" Kort asked.

"Yes, you will finally take your place at my side, but not without my children and not if the embarrassment of their escape is spread across the galaxy."

"It will be done," Kort said. "I'll begin preparations for banding right away and have my most trusted people assembled as a crew by morning."

TWELVE

The aromas that struck Spin the moment she moved through the entryway of the Three Rivers Palace made her hungry within seconds. It was busy, with patrons standing at a long counter ordering hot dumplings, noodles and rice with vegetables and chicken from half a dozen human cooks. You watched them make your food with only a transparent barrier between you and your preparer.

The walls were painted gold, with long, fighting black and red dragons decorating the space. "Spin," said the Governor from a table close to the door. Sitting across from him was the white haired woman who called herself Omira. The Governor smiled at her and pushed his bowl aside. "I'll leave you two to talk."

"I'm glad I met you, Mitchel," she told him as he stood. "Good luck."

"You too, I hope to see you again," the Governor said. He stopped a moment to speak to Spin before leaving. "I believe she's a friend, but she'd tell you to judge for yourself. I'll see you back at the ship."

Spin, her head full of questions, approached the table as Omira got to her feet. The woman was a full head taller than her, wearing a white jacket made of thick, leathery material that ended at her midriff, just long enough to conceal a weapon holstered under her arm. Her top was the same length, leaving her middle bare. Her belt and the tights beneath it were black, leading into thigh high boots that matched her jacket. She greeted Spin with a smile and an embrace so warm that it felt more like a friendly reunion. "I'm glad we have a chance to meet." She noticed Spin glance at her boots and tugged on the top of her left one. "Oh, I saw yours and thought I'd try them. Good armour, but they don't feel practical yet."

"I haven't had a chance to find anything else," Spin said. "It was sort of the best thing in the closet at the time."

"That explains it," Omira said, gesturing for both of them to sit. "You escaped not long ago then, I was wondering, I've met the only other Aspen who managed to break her programming."

"Wait, before we get into that, how are there not a dozen port guards here arresting you?" Spin asked.

"Oh, right. None of their security can see me. We stole a couple primary data nodes and the organization I was doing the job for was able to use them to take control of everything in Midtown. Only the executives and government in charge know about it, but they've been locked out for about an hour now. The last thing I did before I got paid in full was have them wipe out my identity here, so I'm just a normal woman having a normal meal, meeting a few friends."

"So you're not one of the Nays?" Spin asked.

"No, I'm not an anarchist, I just like being where history is happening and getting paid to play a part. I'm a full blown pirate, if you ask the United Core Authority. Don't get me wrong, the Nays are right to mistrust the establishment of an old traditional parliament here, the system they were building is all wrong for a planet with this kind of population, but they're just anarchists. Powerful, well-armed anarchists, but they don't have a plan for what happens after they topple the young establishment here."

"That's what they're all about?" Spin asked.

"Absolutely, and when it's accomplished in an hour or two, because there's no stopping them now, the big problem they have will hit them right where it hurts. They don't have a plan for what happens after they've kicked this government out. In a month, when it's a good time to come back and use this as a safe harbour, I bet it'll be controlled by a dictator, or maybe a few warring dictators. A great place to stop and trade, but you wouldn't want to live here."

"I'm sorry, I have no idea who you are, and we'll get to that, but I have to ask: why did you help them?"

"The price was right, and I saw a way to do it that would put the fewest number of innocent people at risk. You saved the only innocent that was about to die because of our mission, actually. Thank you."

A smiling waiter delivered a bowl of steaming hot udon noodles with vegetables and chicken. Spin looked from the noodles in front of her to him, a little confused. "Fresh broccoli, spring onions, shredded radish and chicken in chicken broth with udon. Madam ordered for you, would you like something to drink?"

"Um, water?" Spin answered. The waiter wasted no time in producing a self-cooling glass filled with clean water.

"Enjoy," he said before returning to his other tables.

"Why am I here?" Spin asked. "I mean, I hate to be blunt, you seem nice – no – amazing, but I have to ask."

Omira laughed and nodded. "You didn't get access to a lot of information about your people, did you? The fabricants, or dolls as some people call us."

"No," Spin said. "I'm surprised the Countess let us learn anything, but she had to explain why we were treated differently from all the other slaves somehow, and she's not particularly creative."

"I've heard the Countess called many things, but uncreative is a new one. Well, I'll get to the point. I'm an after image of who I was, a doll from the Celeste Line. Just like you are from the Aspen Line of dolls, my original existence was the Celeste Line, one whole generation before yours. There were thirty-five of us though, and we were made as life companions, so we didn't have a mate like you do, but, wait, what's wrong?"

Spin realized that whatever levity she had was gone, and Omira must have seen that. "I'm sorry, Larken was killed."

Omira took her free hand, the other was half way to picking up chopsticks, and looked into her eyes. "I'm sorry, I can't imagine how painful that is for you. We have a Nathan aboard who lost his mate two years ago, it's always hard."

"You have another doll crewmate?" Aspen asked.

"That's what I was getting to," Omira said. "Have some noodles, I'll explain."

Spin didn't have to be told twice. There was something

comforting about the woman's confidence, and she hadn't eaten in too long.

"I was a lucky one, when I was a fabrication, I was bonded to a wealthy man in Able's Landing, deep in British Alliance territory. Some of my happiest memories were from the twenty years I spent as an adult with him. My line weren't sold until we were pre-aged to sixteen standard years, and then we were chemically and mentally pre-set to fall in love with them. He introduced me to his family as his second wife, and within the first year there was nowhere else I'd rather be. He treated me with respect, and I believe he fell in love with me after a while, real love too. We were happy together for twenty years, his family even accepted me after a while, and then my expiration time came up. Twenty-one years to the day from my time of arrival in his living room. By then I was invaluable to him in business, I had watched some of his grandchildren grow and helped with their care, becoming a granny to five of them even though I didn't look like a granny at all, and I was his life partner. I never felt like a slave, so I was lucky," Omira said.

"It sounds like it," Spin said around a mouthful of noodles.

"He spent a fortune secretly finding a group of researchers and former fabricators, people who made humans from scratch for a living, finding a way to transfer everything that was in that Celeste to an unlimited fabrication, me. They did it, and, without my original knowing, I was made and during some evening near the end, they scanned her in her sleep. There was only one problem. For some reason, when I woke up for the first time, I knew I wasn't the original, and for the first year or so, I can't be sure, I literally went mad because I couldn't wrap my head around being a copy. I thought I was worthless at times, was sure I couldn't live up to who Celeste was at others, and at other times I was unbelievably paranoid, I thought it was some kind of trick, and they'd drop me into a mulching unit any second."

The mental image of Omira being chopped up and recycled made Spin choke a little.

"Sorry, bad wording, but you get my meaning," Omira said. "Celeste's owner, or more like life partner at that point let me see the footage of her passing. With his family around her treating her like one of their very own, she passed away, and he was devastated. My recovery began there, and before long we realized that I knew I should love him, but I didn't. I had all of Celeste's thoughts and memories, but I didn't feel like her. He didn't feel the same about me either, so he never revealed me to his family. I also had a fascination with Celeste's origin, and the fabrications. With his level of access, I was able to find out about all the new models the companies were making – you and Larken included – and through Celeste's memories of his friends outside of the British Alliance, where slavery was legal, I could recall how most dolls were treated. Many were like Celeste, companions to widows and widowers. More of them were slaves of every kind in high class society."

"How did your master get away with having Celeste so long in British territory?" Spin asked.

"He had a fake history made for her, it was iron clad, and she didn't look exactly like all the other Celeste Models. If you look me up using my original name, you'll find I'm her daughter of record. Omira is a name I took later, when the big question came up. I was still in hiding when I asked him if I was free, if I could just leave. When I learned that the door was always open,

I started preparing to go. A few months later I left, that was about eighteen years ago, and he's gone now. His eldest daughter and son were killed when the virus hit an artificial intelligence piloting their shuttle. He passed away not long after."

Spin could see Omira was still mourning her old master, regardless of which generation she was. "I'm sorry," she told her.

"It's the human way," Omira said, flashing a smile. "But fabrications like you have another problem. Your clock is ticking, and you're getting closer to accessing more of your potential all the time. That's the curse of fabrications, we only get better with age, it's part of the marketing. Smarter, endlessly healthy, and more attractive until the last three days, then you get sick and pass away gently. They designed dolls to die at their best so the idea of buying an adult replacement is natural, nearly irresistible for anyone with a little bit of a God complex. I know, I remember everything right up until the last week that Celeste lived through and I'm still trying to be as smart, as charming, and funny as she was. They took away my expiration date, but I think a little potential went away with it too. Genetics are a bitch to figure out when you're building a human from scratch."

"So you're saying I'm only going to get better with time," Spin said. "I've never heard that."

"Most of your people haven't, why would any master tell their slave that they're getting cleverer? None of the fabrications on my crew knew that until I found them, and told them."

"You have people like me on your crew?"

"Five limited editions now, about as rare as you are. We had six, she was an Aspen, she expired last week."

Omira didn't say that offhandedly, though she tried not to

show how painful it was to say. Spin could see that the Aspen she lost meant a lot to her, that almost overshadowed another, more important realization. "Last week. All the Aspens were released within seven months of each other."

"I know, I think you might be the last, it's likely. I'd get scanned, if I were you. Just in case you thought you had more time."

"I thought I did," Spin said, glad she got through most of her noodles before losing her appetite.

"You might, you could have six more months left. I have a scanner on my ship that could tell you for sure," Omira said. "That's one of the reasons why I had to meet you, Mitchel made it easy, otherwise I don't know if I'd have time to invite you to join the crew of the Empress."

"Your ship?" Spin asked. She'd heard of the Empress, it was known as a pirate ship, but she knew little beyond that. "I have friends who need to do something first." The thought of joining another crew, leaving her friends behind and not punishing Captain White felt completely wrong. "I have to do something first, especially if I have less time than I thought left."

"You have to make sure they'll be all right," Omira said. "I understand. They'd be welcome to join too, but our course is set from here. I can't go into too much detail, but we'll be freeing slaves this month. The payday from the job we just finished will keep us going for a while, so we're going to be freeing a lot of people before we have to earn again."

"I want to go with you," Spin said. "I do, it sounds like the right thing to do with the rest of my life, but I owe the people I'm with. If it wasn't for me, none of them would have been marked as slaves, and people they love wouldn't have been killed."

"What happens because of slavery is never the fault of the slave. It's always the fault of the master," Omira said.

"I know, but still," Spin shrugged. "I can't leave them, and I don't think they'd want to abandon our plans."

"I understand. I'll leave you an ident number to call in case things change or if you'd like to call me for any reason. It's been good meeting you, it was important to me that I did, and I'm not disappointed."

"It was good meeting you too," Spin replied, accepting the woman's outstretched hand. It was gently held, not shaken. "Good luck." Then a thought occurred to her. "Oh! I have information about Geist, and the whole manufacturing block there. The labs, the training facilities, everything."

Omira was shocked. "What? Where did you get that?"

"The Countess is planning an expedition there, it was in the database and Larken had a copy of everything. I'll give you her plans, the scouting data and the rest of the research on the mission." She hurriedly brought the files together on the interface lighting up on her forearm and sent it to Omira's device.

"I can't believe this, it could be a while before we figure out how to use this information, but I know it's going to help sometime. I'll make sure no one knows who gave it to me."

"No, make sure everyone knows who gave it to you," Spin said. "If I'm not going to be around long, I'd like people to know Larken and I led people there so no one else could reopen the facilities."

Omira smiled as she stood, Spin did the same and was embraced warmly by the woman. "You're so special, Spin, thank you. The moment you change your mind about joining us, you call my ident. Even if you have two dozen people with you, we'll make it work. You promise, okay?"

Spin was only half released from the embrace when she looked up at Omira. "I promise." Then she saw a tear in Omira's eye and understood. "You and the other Aspen were close."

"I've never loved anyone more," Omira whispered, trying her best to keep her composure. "She only saw me as a friend, but it was enough for me most of the time."

Without hesitation, Spin pulled Omira close and held her tightly. "I'm sure she loved you too," she whispered. They remained together for long enough for people to start staring, then to respectfully avert their eyes.

"Okay, we have to go," Omira said. "We have about twenty minutes before Midtown goes to hell."

"Thank you for everything," Spin said.

"Thank you, Spin. We'll see each other again."

THIRTEEN

Sleep was difficult to find. Memories of Larken came to Spin the moment her head landed on the pillow. Those memories were surrounded by a coterie of emotions. Anger, sadness, regret, and other minor players chased sleep away. Worry wasn't far behind, she had to get scanned and find out how much time she really had left.

How and when she finally got to sleep was uncertain, but eventually she drifted off and managed to catch a few hours. Spin would miss the bed in the luxury transport, its high level of comfort was probably the only reason she was able to sleep. A quick look at the display hovering over her arm told her that she had been asleep for nearly five hours, but it felt more like five minutes.

Her personal computer warned her that there was a crew meeting scheduled in twenty-five minutes and she rolled out of bed then walked straight to the shower. The water was perfect, one of the trademarks of a good luxury transport, and another thing Spin would miss in the future, she was sure. There was no way they could use the ship as a real home base. It had some armour, but not enough, and it was lightly armed at best – except for the missiles, but that was a small thing compared to the ships most crews used when they expected trouble. There was the problem of the thing being immediately identifiable by sight, it didn't matter how many times she changed the transponder signal. Anyone who had been near one of the Countess' transports would recognize it as one of hers immediately, it's headless duck shape was a dead giveaway, even if it was painted, which would take time, something that she felt she had little of.

The shower stall switched to dryer mode, and vibrated the water off her skin while warm air blasted her body. It was time to face her fate, she decided. As soon as she was finished drying, she picked up the medical scanner she borrowed from the medical compartment on her way to bed the night before and pointed it at herself. It worked silently for a moment, then sent the results to the computer bonded with the skin on her left arm.

Her health was perfect. "Life expectancy?" she asked.

"Three months, nine days and approximately two hours," it replied.

"What?" shrieked Mirra from the other side of the door.

Spin hurriedly got into her blue consuit, thankful for the smooth fabric, and that it had cleaned itself automatically. "Mirra, you can't say anything," she said as she got the lower half on and slit the hatch open. "I don't want anyone to know."

"What? Why?" Mirra asked. "We should try to find you

help, see if there's someone out there who knows how to fix this."

"Listen," Spin said. "I thought I had time for that, but now I know I have enough time to try to save myself, or to set my friends up so I know they'll be in a good way when I'm gone. Do you understand? Everyone I care about is in danger right now, and it's because of me."

"No, not me," Mirra said. "You saved me, you saved Della, so we're already in better shape than we were before you met us. Everyone else on this ship seems to be able to take care of them-selves, well, except for Nigel, but he has Sun and maybe even the Governor. You have to stop looking at yourself as a cause of burden."

"Fine, I'll work on that, but don't tell anyone, at least not for now. We need to focus on getting a better ship, set up with a larger crew. Then, when we're in a position of strength, I'll tell them, okay?"

"Don't wait too long," Mirra said.

"You promise you'll keep it a secret," Spin said.

"I do, I promise."

Spin sighed. "Why are you here, anyway?" she asked more light-heartedly.

"I was going to help you through your morning. You know, get you dressed, brushed and ready for your day."

"You don't have to do that," Spin said, realizing that she hadn't finished putting her suit on, so she resumed, slipping her arm into a sleeve.

"Don't I?" Mirra said, helping her with the rest of her suit then closing the consuit most of the way up the front. "Besides, it's a force of habit. Della's kicked Nigel out of her cabin and is already helping our Captain."

"What?" Spin asked as she slipped her foot into her boot with Della's assistance.

"Oh yes, Della is absolutely not a lesbian. She didn't signal one way or another the whole time we were serving together, but now that she's free, apparently Nigel's her type. I walked in on them last night."

"I really thought you two might have found something." The second boot went on and Mirra held up a brush, which Spin didn't even see her pick up. "I can do that," she said. Mirra put Spin in a chair, stuck a chocolate meal bar into her mouth and started brushing. Spin felt like she was ten years old all over again.

"I sort of hoped, but that ended in an awkward talk where Della explained how wonderful we fit together as friends. Then she suggested I consider dating the Governor."

"That doesn't make sense," Spin said around a mouthful of chocolate flavoured nutrient bar. "Unless you're closer to the middle of the spectrum?"

"Well, I can appreciate a handsome man, but I don't think I could love one that way. Now, if Sun were interested, I most definitely would. That's a secret you can keep."

"I will. So, Sun, really?" Spin asked.

"That porcelain skinned, dark haired goddess? Absolutely. Even if she wasn't lovely, her confidence would draw me in. Why do you think I'm here taking care of you?"

"Oh, so if you have a crush on someone it's inappropriate," Spin said.

"Exactly. I can be friends and take care of you professionally without worrying. You remind me of an adorable woodland creature," Mirra said.

"I am not a chipmunk, I am a human being," Spin chuckled. It wasn't the first time someone compared her to some small, cute mammal.

"You see my point, I don't fall for 'adorable' so I'm a great fit for your helper, or carer, whatever."

"You know; you don't have to worry about having a place on the crew if you want one. It's not a worry, you don't even need to do any of this if you don't want to."

"Della and I are very good at it, and it turns out we don't mind doing it as long as we're getting paid and are free to leave. Besides, I've heard that if we're not busy doing other things, we'll be scraping platinum foil off the walls."

"Ah, you might have to do some of that anyway," Spin said. "It's probably going to be easier than you think."

"There's that at least."

Spin let Mirra finish help her get ready, and it did go faster, she even ended up wearing a little makeup by the end, something she wouldn't have bothered to do for herself. "So, today is going to be hard? Maybe dangerous?" Mirra said as the pair left the compartment.

"Yes, and probably yes," Spin replied quietly.

THE GOVERNOR WAS SITTING with Dorian in the passenger seating in the middle of the ship. Nigel, Sun and Della were right behind Spin as she entered the main cabin. "We're in a hurry this morning," Sun announced. "I'll get this meeting over with quickly so we can have a real breakfast. It might be one of the last of the like that we'll have in a while, since the ingredients we have here aren't common."

Della didn't sit down, but kept walking to the galley. On the way there she passed Leland, who was about to open a meal bar and she snatched it from his fingers. He shrugged and sat down with the rest of the crew. Spin watched everyone else take their seats, then the cockpit door at the top of the short stair opened to admit a dark haired man almost as short as she was. She'd forgotten about him, Jorin, who was one of the slaves she rescued from the fungal pools. One of his cheeks was still thickly caked with treatment cream. He nodded and smiled at her briefly before taking a seat. "Our night watch pilot, Jorin," Sun said. "He did a fine job, considering it was his first watch on a ship."

"Ever," he said. "I mostly watched the console from a safe distance just in case any of the displays turned red and kept my hand over the alert button."

"There's three quarters of the job, right there," Dorian said. "Well done."

"Right. Let's get to it," Sun said. "We're headed to Vernon, an unregulated town outside of the main planetary port. Last night, Nigel finished work on the ship's protective net, so if anyone or anything touches the hull while the hatches are closed, they'll be burned to slag."

"Just fixed a few severed lines, they got cut when the ship was hit aft," he explained.

"That's going to keep the ship safe with most of you inside while Spin, Nigel and I go see our old captain. We'll be scouting him out first, seeing if we can't connect with a few people we know are trustworthy on the crew. From there it can go one of two ways."

"Wait, I'm going with you, right? I have a debt to settle with White too," Dorian said.

"We'll settle our issue first, since it's our best way in. If we can connect with friendly crewmembers from the Cool Angel, then we can force a vote for Captain."

"And you'll put yourself up as a replacement?" Dorian asked. "They won't go for that, not if Keith or Denise are still there. Keith is next in line as White's First Mate and Denise is the favourite Lieutenant."

"Right, there's a chance the vote won't go my way, but that's slim. Captain White and his lieutenants sold us out, there's no way his lieutenants didn't know about this before or shortly after it happened, and if they found out about it shortly after, the rest of the crew would force them to hold a vote to get rid of White."

"Don't be so sure," Dorian said. He threw his hands up defensively in response to Sun's scowl. "Just sayin', it's a greedy crew over there."

"Right, so while we're here, the priority is to get the ship ready to sell. Mirra will lead you all in a round of cleaning and light repairs. If you don't know how to do something, then ask about it. The Governor used to fly several of his own personal craft when he was at home, so he'll be in the cockpit listening in on us in case anything goes sideways. Any questions?"

"I thought she was Captain?" Jorin asked, pointing at Spin.

"She's our sponsor, the one with the money and the brains that got us together. She made me captain, and reserved the position of second in command for herself."

"Ah, okay," he replied. "Lots to learn."

"If there's nothing else, then let's get to the galley, Della's serving berry pancakes and something with oranges and grapefruit that I've never heard of but it sounds delicious," Sun said.

Spin couldn't help but notice that Dorian was the last to stand and join the group. Even through synthetic skin, she could see his frustration.

FOURTEEN

"I wish we'd spent more time off ship while you were in my service," Sun said to Spin as they made their way through the chaotic market that had grown up around the rough port. Hundreds of kilometers had been sectioned off by Urono Enterprises, then divided with scrap metal fencing into different sized sections for a variety of ship classes. Roads were left between them and that's where a seemingly endless number of merchants tried to sell and trade.

There was a digital trade board, but when Spin checked it she found the system was clogged with scammers, spammers and advertisers. The data wasn't even worth looking at unless you knew exactly what you were looking for. There were people buying ships, however, but they paid a tenth of the value or less, their poor damaged transport wouldn't go for much if they traded or sold where they were. "I'm getting the feeling that I'll have an accelerated education from here on out," Spin said as she stepped around a pile of condensation coils and cables still in their package, but piled at a vendor's feet in the dirt.

"Have you found any of the banks you need here?" Sun asked.

Spin checked and nodded. "The Bur-Shuk have a major branch here, they could probably pay me in about ten hours. Doesn't look like I'll lose much to transaction fees either."

"Do you think Della and Mirra will want to stick around after you've paid them?"

Spin and Nigel flinched as a low flying shuttle passed overhead. "Della will probably follow Mirra, and I think she'll stick around. She really wants to find her place in the crew. I don't know if she'll stick around if we join the Cool Angel's crew unless you're made captain."

"You don't believe in this plan," Sun said.

"I don't know, what Captain White did was against the faith of the crew," Spin replied.

"I think maybe we just can't call it right now," Nigel said as he stepped around a puddle only to drop his foot into a thick patch of mud. "Right?"

"Right, but I think it's worth pursuing. Most of the crew who didn't know White betrayed us will be on our side, I think."

What would you do?" Sun asked.

Spin thought for a moment then shook her head. "Your way is the most peaceful way, but the only captain the Cool Angel has ever had is White, right? So I don't know how that's going to affect things either."

"If the crew wants him gone, they want him gone. He can't do much if no one will follow orders," Nigel said.

"You have a point." A sour, sulphurous smell filled the air, and thanks to Nigel's disgusted expression Spin could see she wasn't the only one who caught it. Rain followed a moment later, and her suit provided a deep hood for her to hide in. The smell remained.

"From grey skies to grey rain, isn't this place wonderful?" Nigel asked.

Most of the vendors along the side of the muddy road either had a makeshift umbrella or retreated entirely, returning to whatever shelter they came from. Sun walked to one who was selling a variety of communicators and pointed to a tiny packaged communicator. "How much for the Blip Pod?"

"Three plat," the vendor said.

"Here's a pip," Sun said, handing him a real piece of currency instead of outlaw minted platinum pieces. "That good?"

"Here," he said, handing her the tiny package.

Sun handed it to Spin. "Turn that on and find out if it'll uplink to any UCA ships in the area. We have to know if they're here."

Spin did exactly as she was told; unwrapped the flat pill shaped communicator, turned it on and tried to register it on the Unitec Core Authority network and immediately found a node. Using her computer as an interface but blocking all identifying markers, she did a search for the strongest signals. "I see five ships on this hemisphere. Four of them are small corvettes, looks like they're on the ground, and there's a bigger ship in orbit."

"Okay, now do a quick search for any of the Cool Angel's crew, please."

Spin did so, and was surprised to see the results come back so quickly. "I think the UCA are connected with the major communications networks here. Whoever runs this place might be happy they're here. Got the results and saved them on my comm though."

Sun took the communicator, turned it off, then handed it to the vendor. "My friend doesn't like it," she told him.

"You open package, you keep it. No refund with open package," the vendor said nonchalantly.

"Sure, just sell it to someone else then," Sun said as she pressed it into his hand. "No refund necessary." The trio moved on, slogging through the deepening muck. "He'll sell that thing in a heartbeat or burn it quick. Either way, if the UCA decide to track it, we'll be long gone. This does give us a reason to hurry this along. Let's get out of the rain," Sun said.

"A pip or plat for new legs? A pip or plat for new legs?" a man asked as he moved through the pedestrians in the middle on a beaten hover board. He held a cup up to them as they passed, only a little higher than waist height but politely.

SPIN STOPPED him and held her hand over his cup so he couldn't see what she was about to drop in. "Is there a shuttle stand nearby?"

"Shuttle stand?" he asked. "No end of shuttles, Miss, no drivers for 'em. Hopper's is right there, past that plank walk. You buy a shuttle for nothin', pay what you would for a ride in some places."

"I'm Spin," she told him, dropping five pips into his cup, a donation worth ten or more rough minted platinum. "If I give you my ident, can you be my eyes around here?"

He looked into his cup, then back at her. "You got a friend

on Valour Row," he replied. "Name's Tiber. Anything unusual happens here, I'll pass the word to you."

"Thank you," Spin said, passing him a temporary identification number. "There will be more pips in it for you later."

The trio made their way to the next corner as Tiber sought shelter in a rough lean-to made from old metal plating. "You're better at being off ship than I thought," Sun said. "I never saw that kind of thinking when you were in my service."

"Making friends everywhere, it's cool," Nigel said.

"It's how I survived while I was homeless, made friends with the right people, and made sure that they knew I was thinking about their well-being," Spin replied. "I'd like to take credit, but it usually comes naturally."

"It's a good thing, just be careful with how much money you put out there," Sun said. "That kind of cash isn't always going to be easy to come by."

"With the information I have on the Countess, I can't agree," Spin said. The trio stepped onto a sidewalk made from felled trees and started heading for a bright red sign that said Hopper's Ships & Repair that hung above a heavy steel door. The rest of the building looked like a tall two storey bunker. "Tell me how much money and what kind of risk you're willing to take for it, and I'll set you up with a mark. With the ship we have, we're limited, but there are targets we can hit. No, money isn't the problem, being conspicuous, vulnerable, that's our problem with the Fleet Feather." A nagging thought that she should be more careful about how she spoke to Sun, since she was much more experienced and her former boss, was acknowledged and ignored.

"We are under crewed though," Nigel offered.

"Not at all. There are targets that we could hit where using muscle would blow the whole operation. The smartest objectives we could choose right now are the ones where we don't have to fire a shot, where we use our brains to get in, and get out before anyone even realizes we're not supposed to be there." Off the top of her head, Spin could think of several corporate colonies and operations where that was true, and she was beginning to enjoy thinking about her former master's assets as potential targets.

"You've been holding out on us," Sun said. "I'm impressed."

"You shouldn't be, I helped manage the Countess' affairs and relationships for years. There are allies who don't even know what she looks like, they only did serious business through me. The problem we really have is time. The longer we wait, the less accurate my intelligence is, and the more people know I've escaped again."

"I realize that," Sun said. "It's the same with all intelligence, really. The older it gets the less reliable it is."

"Yes, but if I get my hands on any computer connected to the Countess' corporate network, I can get more. Even if they change the passcodes, I know how they're generated, I know what I can get into without them. Straight up cash is the hardest thing to get to, but if you want supplies, work sites so you can free more people like us, or hardware of almost any kind, then that's a lot easier. The shipping routes don't change often, neither do work sites or where they need heavy transports or large building equipment."

"What would we do with that kind of hardware?" Nigel asked as they passed through the metal doors.

"Look behind you," Spin said. "From the looks of this place, it used to be some kind of forest, and they made it a divided lot so they could sell the space for landing ships. I'm sure whoever runs it would pay for heavy excavation equipment or mass recyclers so they could make some of the space better, maybe create a premium area."

"Man, that is good thinking. Wouldn't fit in our hold though," Nigel said.

"Creating a need where there was none before," said a short, stout woman from behind the counter. "If you've come with heavy equipment, then I can set you up with someone whose looking."

"We're just looking to rent a shuttle. I'm Sun," she offered her hand.

"Well, I could rent you something reliable, or sell you something you'll keep forever. I'm Thenna Bruce, one of the sales people on the floor here." She opened a pair of double doors to reveal a large hangar with dozens of polished craft inside. At a glance it was obvious that many of them were reconditioned, but some actually looked new.

"I'm afraid buying anything legitimately is off the table," Sun whispered. "We'll pay a little more to take something from your backlot though."

"Not necessary," Thenna said with a large smile. "We are not only registered with the Core Authority, but with the British Alliance, and they don't care that you've slipped someone's leash. The registration will take a couple weeks to get legitimized by the British, but it'll be legitimate. No extra charge."

Spin inwardly cursed herself for not thinking of the loophole. In the British Alliance territories slavery was illegal, and anyone could own property. It didn't occur to her that an escaped slave could simply register ownership of ships with them instead of the Core Authority. It didn't change the illegality of owning a ship in the Core Authority territory, but it made it possible for them to buy a ship legally.

"In that case, we'll probably leave here today with something," Sun said. "Just a basic planet hopper though."

"Are you sure? We have an orbital shipyard if you're looking for something more extensive."

"Just something we can use to get around locally without drawing attention."

"What are we looking for in terms of armaments, then? I got five combat shuttles ready to go, maybe within your budget?"

Spin was keenly aware that she had over thirty thousand in United Core World Currency slips on her, and that wasn't including a pile of pips and smaller slips she had in a small pocket in her boot. "Does the Port Authority watch for armed shuttles?"

"No, check with anyone, anything we have here is too small for them to worry over. It's the corvettes and over-powered blockade breakers that they keep their eye on. Are we expecting trouble?"

"We're trying to keep a low profile," Sun said.

"Well, then I think I know what you should see," Thenna said, walking them to a sleek looking four-person shuttle with faded paint. It had been polished, but aside from that it was fairly non-descript.

Spin couldn't help but look around the hangar. Some of the ships were converted robot transports, maintenance and storage bays repurposed for seating and other conveniences. The largest of the ships within the hangar were fairly pedestrian, two old sky busses, and a light military transport that looked older than all three of them combined.

"Hey," Nigel said, tapping her on the shoulder and nodding towards a longer seven-person ship. It had a sleek narrow wing look and a half deck that Spin guessed had some sleeping or storage space over the aft half. "That's a Pearson Long Runner. I've seen them before. It's a good model. A little shielding, some sleeping pods, a couple guns. That's going to be handy."

"Probably expensive," Spin said, looking at the blacked out transparent metal portholes and view shields along the front. The clean grey and blue finish looked fresh, most likely recently restored.

"I see your crewmates have spotted a real bargain," Thenna declared as she shuffled over to the Long Runner. "Long boat to minor military organizations and scout ship to many governments. I can give you a good price on this one."

"We're not looking for something overly permanent," Sun countered.

"That would fit in the Fleet Feather's hold," Nigel whispered to her. "If we lock it down to the damaged side. It's the best thing here."

"Which one of you is the mechanic?" asked Thenna, looking at Nigel. "You can take a look, no problem."

"Hell yes," he said, nearly running to the shuttle's side hatch. "I mean, I will perform a cursory inspection, you know, just in case my Captain is interested."

"It might be more than we need," Sun said. "More expensive too."

"But you will gain in security. This ship has light military

class armour from one end to the other, combat class manoeuvring thrusters and it has been completely reupholstered, from
the pilot's seat to the bedding. Sleeping space for seven, with
pull out tables and seating space for everyone. Oh, and we've
restored one of the best features." She snapped her fingers and
two turreted pairs of small cannons slipped out of their conceal-
ment doors from the top and bottom of the ship. "Scythe guns,
firing tiny molten slugs surrounded by a high energy jolt. Just in
case you need a little protection. There's a small missile
launcher in the front too, but we're not allowed to load that
here."

Nigel disappeared into the shuttle. Knowing him he'd be
able to assess the ship in less than ten minutes. "How much?"
Sun asked.

"Fifty-five thousand, and I'll throw in our twenty-day guarantee on all parts for free. That'd normally run you sixty-five
thousand total, so you're saving big. You realize, this is no starter
ship, it's the kind of thing you use for years and years."

"I can see that," Sun said. "What if I take that basic runner
over there?" She pointed at a blocky five person shuttle several
spots over.

"You really are talking basic, there," Thenna said. "Nothing
wrong with it, but there are no frills, just good for land-
hopping."

"How much?"

"We sell those all the time for eight-nine-nine-nine."

"Ah," Sun said. She looked to Spin who was disappointed at
the large price tag of both ships. The blocky basic vessel should
have been much lower, even with her limited experience she
could see that. The larger, flashier Long Runner seemed pricy

too, it was more than what she had with her, but she knew that armed ships always came at a premium. So much so that many owners spent a great deal of time and effort on arming ships they bought without weaponry preinstalled. "There are a lot of ships we can look at between these two extremes," Sun told her.

Spin's response was almost instinctive. Instead of answering Sun, she looked to another salesperson who wasn't with a customer and asked; "There are other dealerships nearby, aren't there?" in a loud voice.

He looked at her, then to Thenna who seemed alarmed, then back to Spin. "None like this, Ma'am."

"All right, how about I make you a deal. The Long Runner has a lot of man hours in it for restoration, but I bet I can convince the boss to let it go for twenty-eight thousand. I can only offer our five-day warranty at that price though, extending it will cost a little more. That's a great deal considering the peace of mind you'll have with the protection you're buying."

"Nigel? How is it going in there?" Sun asked.

He emerged with a stormy expression. "Everything scans all right, it's built well, but we have problems. The main combat shield generator is gone. They've got a hopped up manoeuvring shield installed instead. The shields might take a few micro-meteor hits, but that's it. They restored everything inside this ship except for the missile launcher, I wouldn't trust it until it's completely rebuilt. Oh, and instead of a wormhole generator they've installed a bunch of empty drawers."

"Could you rebuild the missile launcher?"

"Sure, give me a space I can work in and a week," he replied. "Other than those problems, it's a good space worthy ship, no chinks in the armour."

"Nine thousand for the Long Runner," Sun said.

"I'd be taking a loss," Thenna replied.

"The wormhole generator is something I'd have to replace, my machinist is going to have to rebuild the missile launch system, and we'll need new shields if we keep the ship for any length of time. What's the cost on that, you figure, Nigel?"

"At a guess, we're talking twenty, maybe twenty-five thousand platinum?" he said with a shrug. "That's with new parts, used you're still over twelve thousand, I'm pretty sure."

"So," Sun said. "We started high, I figure without a warranty and those parts in the price, I'd feel good about paying eleven thousand."

"I can go as low as nineteen thousand."

"No warranty, and seventeen-five."

"On second thought, I think I'll just take that boat," Sun said, thumbing at the boring, blocky ship. "I'll give you four thousand for it. No warranty, we're not staying in range long."

Thenna was fully put off her sales game, and she was stuck looking from the impressing Long Runner to the blocky land hopper. "What if I gave you – and it is a gift – the Long Runner for fourteen-five."

"What if we paid in UCA marked currency?" Sun said.

"Then it's fourteen thousand," Thenna said, her eyes lighting up.

"It's eight thousand, or we leave," Sun said. "And we buy a ship with its original shield unit intact."

"Nine thousand is the best I can do, even for hard coded plat," Thenna said. "And we'll all be happy at that price."

"Nigel," Sun said. "Is there any reason why I shouldn't take that deal?"

"Get a five-day warranty, just in case we pull the trigger on those guns and a flag on a stick comes out," he said.

"Deal?" Sun asked Thenna.

"Done," Thenna replied. The moment they finished shaking hands, she was off checking to make sure everything that was supposed to come with the ship was inside. Nigel and Sun were right behind her, checking the interior.

Spin looked inside and was fairly satisfied. It wasn't like the luxury craft she grew up seeing, but it was nice. There were three pull out beds on the main level that doubled as seating when they were folded up, and five in the upper compartment. There was enough storage and room for people to run the small turrets inside as well. Someone like Nigel would have to duck often enough, but Sun and Spin would fit with room to spare. She stopped another sales person as he passed. He was extremely clean, and wore a long suit coat over a formal shirt with frills. "I'm wondering; do you have an interstellar ship lot here with armed vessels?"

"Combat ready?" he asked quietly, so Thenna couldn't hear. "We just finished working on one, we have five available."

"What's your cheapest one like?" she asked.

"It's not what I'd call cheap," he said with a smile that revealed a row of nickel plated teeth. "They're all high-end, but refurbished, so low prices. The lowest is a North Star Company Surge Twelve Hundred. Can take a crew of thirty-five, medium combat armour, rank fifteen shields but we could upgrade that for you if you need it, and it has five ball turrets. Each turret has twin particle pulsers – Claw Nine Hundreds, they'll make a mess of any Starfighter or tear up some bigger hull. One rotary railgun that can fire just iron, junk rounds or specialty rounds if you know how to make 'em. It's a great ship on its own, even better if you have someone who can make improvements later. There's room for modifications."

"How much?" Spin asked.

"Nineteen million plat," he replied. "Good price for a small reaver, you can take a lot on with that."

Spin was a little taken aback by the price, and by his frankness in what he expected her to use it for. "Would you do one point nine?" she asked.

"You know what? If you can pay with UCA credits, then I'll go as low as one point four. No dickering, you fly off today. I'll even give you five days' warranty. Think about it, it's a good deal," he said before sending her his ident and slinking off before Thenna could notice him making a deal with her customers. "It's the Gunman," he whispered before he was out of earshot.

"What's that about?" Nigel asked in a whisper.

"Just finding out how deep I'd have to go into my finances to buy a ship, just in case things don't go well with the Cool Angel."

"Did you ask him about trading in?" Nigel asked.

"No, I just wanted a price on our most affordable option," she said, aware that Sun was noticing that they were having their own conversation while she was being shown the details of the ship. "Shush, it wasn't serious."

"Can you check to see if any of our old friends are around? Especially Hugo," Sun asked.

"Yes Ma'am," Spin said, bringing up her old crew list from the Cool Angel to see who was in range. To her surprise, a whole third of the crew were absent, but she managed to find

Hugo, one of the crew's lieutenants. Spin always liked him, and doubted that he knew anything about Captain White betraying his own people. He wouldn't have gone along with that. She waited until Thenna was finished showing Sun the refurbished main control panel before telling her. "Hugo is in range. I can get on closed comms with him."

"Good, let's pay up and set a meeting with him."

FIFTEEN

If the Fleet Feather met a fate like the Solar Queen, then Spin would be beyond pleased. The Solar Queen was a larger luxury vessel than the Fleet Feather, and its owner turned it into a large pub, social club and brothel. From the looks of it, the ship could still fly, but it seemed like it had been permanently docked on a slip that was open to the public.

The main area inside was where most of the people who wanted to meet up seemed to go, with many tables and groups of friends hanging out. Booths offered more privacy, and those patrons seemed quieter. Large doors framed in hand crafted wood led to a quieter area under dim light, The Red Ticket Social Club was clearly spelled above the door in gold letters. Even Spin knew that a red ticket, when stuck to the side of a ship, meant that the vessel was designated for scrap. What the owners were trying to tell their patrons by naming their social club after that, she couldn't guess.

They made their way between the tables and past the bar to

those doors and were stopped by two thickly muscled, two and a half meter tall Nafalli. "Thuu," one said, holding his hand up.

"It's all right, they're with me," Hugo said as he opened one of the doors from the other side. "Come on in."

The social club was a stark contrast to the pub behind them. The matching tables were made of wood, the chairs were padded, and the bar featured bottles from around the galaxy. Scantily clad servants of both sexes made their way between tables quietly delivering sizzling plates, exotic drinks and leading a few patrons up a set of wooden stairs that was inlaid with platinum features. "We're over here," Hugo said, leading Sun, Spin and Nigel to a quiet, well-padded booth. Spin noticed that Nigel's jaw had dropped and it didn't look like it was going to rise any time soon, and she gently pushed his chin up with a finger.

"Sorry, I've just never seen a place like this," he whispered.

"S'okay, it's not as amazing as it seems, trust me," Spin replied with a smile.

Before Sun could sit down, Hugo embraced her, his larger frame enveloping her with care. "I was sure you were all in prison or worse." He offered a hug to Spin and she accepted his warm gesture, laughing when he pulled Nigel into the fold so he could squeeze both of them at once. "The Angel hasn't been the same since you left. Where's Trevor and Boro?"

"They were killed," Sun said, not softening the blow. "White took a bounty from the UCA, and they sold us to a corporate slaver outfit run by a Countess. You've heard of her."

"What? White sold you out?" Hugo said as he took a seat in the booth. "That's a better explanation for what's been going on. White paid everyone a share and disbanded the lower ranks of his crew. Offered his Lieutenants and Chiefs a buyout too, I was thinking of taking it. But there were no bounties on you," he said to Sun.

"I'm an escaped limited run custom fabrication," Spin said. "I'm one of two of the Countess' dolls."

"That explains the money. White told us he sold the Lunar Leaper to pay for the refit, but that seemed a little off. What he's been spending is a lot more than what he'd get for an armed cargo hauler. He's been keeping to himself too."

"Now you know why," Sun said. "I want to force a vote, White doesn't deserve the Angel, or to command a crew."

"Or to breathe," Spin said before she could stop herself.

Hugo was surprised by the remark, but seemed amused just the same. "Well, that's in order, isn't it? If it were anyone other than you, Sun, I'd expect you to come at him sideways, put him in braces while he slept or slit his throat, but a vote to get him gone makes more sense. The problem is, there aren't many low ranking crew left. Everyone who you could sway easily already got a cut of the profits from our last run and they're who-knows-where."

"You can recall anyone who's still on the planet. If the Lieutenants agree that anyone White paid off can still vote because this happened while they were still working for him, then I know we'll have the majority for getting him out," Sun said. "They'll come back if you ask them."

Even Spin knew that Hugo was well liked. He was once with the Carthan Marines, and had a better understanding of how to run a crew than most people she'd met. It didn't help that he was a square-jawed, blue eyed, dark skinned man with a beard that he kept neatly shaved in thin lines. He was an interesting man to look at, and she'd caught herself staring more than once during her service. More than that, he was generally likeable and always fair. "You're right, but we have another problem. You have to stay in your seat after I tell you. Don't do anything about this right now."

"What is it?" Sun asked.

"Keith Daniels has stayed on as White's First Officer, he's upstairs right now," he told her quietly.

"There's no way White's right hand man didn't know he was selling us out," Sun said, shifting one foot out from under the table.

"We'll need him, if this vote is going to stick. The crew will need someone on hand that they can punish. I'm sure just getting him off the crew won't be enough for you either, considering what he cost you."

"Revenge is a luxury," Spin said. "If we want the Cool Angel to come out of this with the right commander at the helm, with the right vision for the crew, we have to focus on that, not revenge."

"Can you seriously guarantee that you won't try to kill Captain White or Keith if I put you all in the same room?"

"You can," Sun said. "What Spin said is exactly right, but if they run they're fair game."

"I don't know if I can agree to that, we might have to convince them to-" before he could finish his sentence Sun was out of her seat, running towards the stairs.

Spin did her best to keep up while trying to figure out what triggered her, and barely caught sight of Keith Daniels, the First Officer of the Cool Angel as he ducked through a side door half way up the staircase. Spin wasn't specifically angry at the First

Officer when she was sitting in the booth, but as she burst through the door, catching up to Sun, she realized that seeing him run made her furious.

The emergency door they passed through let out into a long, dark corridor, and Keith made excellent time. He pulled a tall rack, a buffing machine, and a large trash can into his back trail while running as fast as he could. Sun managed to dodge and overcome all but a pile of buckets, where she tripped over one and fell into the rest. "I'm all right, get him!" she shouted as Spin leapt over her and the mess. "Alive!"

Spin saw him rush through a door and followed him without hesitation. A bolt of energy passed over head as soon as she was through, the door closed. She stopped, held her hands up and cursed herself for not looking before following. They were on the dockside wall of the large commerce building, standing on an emergency catwalk that overlooked a large, empty dry dock, the biggest concrete and metal hangar she'd ever seen. Several workers were cleaning the floor below, and they looked smaller than ants from the dizzying height of the walkway. "All right!"

"Who the fuck are you? I know your friend, but I don't think I've ever seen you before," he said as he kept the weapon levelled at her.

"I'm just her support crewman, I was sucked into all this," she said, trying to angle her face away.

"Wait!" he said, laughing. "Now I see it, you're that girl White found on his ship."

While he continued on, Spin whispered; "Call Dorian, transmit video," to her computer system.

"My God, you have no idea how big of a payday you were.

Wait, how are you here?" He asked anxiously. "They said you belonged to some super power in the sector. How did you get away from that? You realize how much trouble everyone around you is in now? Me, Sun, everyone you're in sight of is in the deepest kind of shit."

"Why did you and White turn me in?" Spin asked.

"You were a marked slave, it was either pack you off on some world somewhere to have a go at life on your own, sell you out like we did, or keep you on board and eventually get arrested for hiding you. Just by being aboard you were screwing us over."

The door burst open behind Spin and Keith fired a warning shot, stopping Sun in her tracks. "There's nowhere to go but down." She said.

A glance over her shoulder revealed that Sun had her sidearm out and was already aiming at Keith. Spin slowly dropped back beside her. "Man, I'm going to get killed!"

A blur of motion streaking from the sky struck Keith like a missile, crushing him to the iron grid of the walkway. "Fucking right," Dorian said from where he straddled Keith. He pounded his trapped quarry twice in the face before Keith's weapon went off. Dorian plucked it from his hand as though he were yanking a dangerous toy from a toddler and tossed it over his shoulder. "Lesson time! Don't turn on your crewmates!" he laughed, pulling an already smoking cigar from his inside jacket pocket and flipping it into his mouth. He took a long draw on the stogie as he got a grip on the man's arm and singled out a hand.

"Dorian, stop! We got him!" Spin said.

"You don't leave them behind," Dorian said, snapping a

bone in Keith's left hand. "You don't turn them in to the UCA," he said as he snapped a second.

Spin rushed to Dorian and kicked him in the side. It was like kicking a concrete pillar. "Stop! We need him in one piece!"

Dorian turned to look at her, his artificial eyes looked crazed, primed for murder. "What?"

"We can't kill him, it'll turn the vote for sure," she said soothingly. "You saved our butts, thank you."

He spat his cigar over the side and stood. "Well, he's not goin' anywhere now. Not on two broken legs. Where do you want him? I'll air lift the snitchy bitch."

"Oh, fuck don't let him take me," Keith said from where he lay awkwardly on the catwalk. He turned his face away from Dorian, cringing.

"Should we get him to the Cool Angel so his people can take care of him, or the Fleet Feather?"

Dorian closed his eyes and seemed to consciously make an effort to focus before nodding.

"I want him in our hands, Leland has the equipment to fix him up. Don't let him out of your sight, he's crafty enough to escape on broken legs, trust me," Sun said.

"What the hell?" asked Hugo from behind them as he came through the door.

Dorian knelt down and gently took Keith in his arms, which still prompted more screaming than anyone, except for maybe Dorian himself, wanted. "Going for a ride, snitch-boy," Spin heard him whisper to Keith. He leapt off the edge of the walkway and took flight across the sky, back towards the Fleet Feather.

"I'm not letting Keith or Captain White walk away from

this," Sun said. "I want them to stand in front of the crew and take whatever payback they think is fair for burning me, burning Spin, burning Nigel and Boro and Trevor and anyone else his greed has touched."

"That's fair, but what I just saw happen was the wrong way to do it, it's punishment before a hearing," Hugo said.

"Is there any way he could justify turning against a Lieutenant and most of the people she's accountable for?" Sun asked.

"But you're using strong arm tactics where the only way to gain trust is through the crew," Hugo said. "You were right to come to me so I could get crewmembers back for this, we need to make them feel like they have a say again, and this treatment of the First Officer goes a long way to damage that trust before you've even gotten started."

Spin understood the sides of the argument, but was more interested in looking past the events. The details of the vote, how it would happen, where it would happen, who would be there and the arrangements of it all didn't interest her. There would be a vote, and people with more experience with her were arranging it.

Nigel burst through the door, out of breath. "Sorry, I did my best to catch up, but got lost a little, what's going on?"

Spin checked her message log with a glance and nodded. "You're coming with me to the new Intergalactic Credit Exchange."

"Oh?" Sun asked.

"You have more details to hammer out here, so we'll go ahead," Spin said. There was also an urgent message from Leland, and it told her not to read it in front of her. Something serious was going on. "You can find your own way back to the Feather?"

"Yes, just run plans like this by me and ask next time."

"Don't worry," Spin said as she passed through the door.

"So I'm going with her?" Nigel asked Sun.

"Yes, make sure she gets where she wants to go, back to the ship and stays out of trouble."

"Aye," Nigel said.

He caught up and walked beside her silently as they walked through the half abandoned commerce centre, a great indoor mall with a transparent ceiling so natural light could cast long shadows and golden shafts. Spin's mind was busy working through the idea that she may only have three months left to live. What would she be able to accomplish? Was there a way to fix the problem? The questions were complicated by a desire for revenge against everyone who was responsible for the capture of her friends and the death of Larken.

"Hey, can I ask why we're headed to an ICE office?"

"I'm sorry, I've been quiet," Spin said, suddenly aware that she had said nothing for the entire twenty-minute walk. "I've been bouncing some money around, and it's finally arrived at a depot where they can give it to me in cash. I have to decide if I'm going to leave it with the Interplanetary Currency Exchanges, or cash out."

"You know what I'd do?" Nigel said. "Pay who I had to pay, take what might get me through some trouble, plus a little fun money, then leave it. Safer there, right?" They boarded their new shuttle and Nigel sat at the controls.

"You're smarter than you look, Nigel."

"That's a compliment, right?" he asked.

"Absolutely," Spin replied.

"Better to look low and dirty on the outside and always be thinking on the inside than to be dirty all the way though," Nigel said offhandedly. She'd heard Boro say the same.

"Before we take off, I have to talk to Leland."

"All right, I'll keep the ship warm."

Spin sat down in the co-pilot seat and called Leland, who answered after several seconds. "Spin, Nigel, how is it going out there?"

"All right, did Dorian get there?" Spin asked.

"Yeah, what a mess. I've got him comfortable now, took a good scan, and I was just about to start setting bones and injecting localized recovery meds."

"We'll let you go so you can get back to it," Spin said.

"No, what I have to tell you won't wait either. I hate to be blunt, Nigel, but unless Spin trusts you with her life, you can't be in the cabin for the next part of the conversation."

Nigel looked to Spin, surprised. "Yeah, that's blunt."

"I trust him," Spin said.

"More than Sun?" Leland pressed.

"I'll just go wait in the back," Nigel said. "No worries, this sounds like the kind of secret I won't be able to hold in anyway." He left and closed the cockpit door behind him.

"All right, what's going on, Leland?"

"I'm keeping a checklist of medical equipment on the ship just so things stay organized in case of an emergency, and found that one of the scanners was missing. I found it in your quarters, that's all right, you had no idea I was obsessing a little over our gear."

"I'll know for next time," Spin said. "Glad you're keeping track though."

"That's not why we have to talk. What I found on it, the details behind the readings and results recorded are a problem. I know you just wanted to find out how much time you have left, and that the results are grim. I'm sorry about that, but I'm sorrier about the cause I found when I looked into the how and why."

He may have been eager to tell her what he found, but Spin could see that now that the moment was upon him, he was afraid to say it aloud. "Tell me, like it's a bandage, just rip it off."

"You know, that's not always the best practice? Sometimes you cause more damage than-" he stopped himself and sighed. "I've looked the results and the records over and over again, there's no other explanation. Sun slipped you an anti-toxin that enhances your immune system against foreign substances. I can only assume that she meant to get the Cetrimemodel out of your system, and it worked, but it also triggered a biological anti-tampering mechanism in your system, costing you eight months. I wouldn't tell you this if I wasn't sure."

"How do you know it was her?" Spin asked, hoping she could prove him wrong in every way.

He brought up a recording from the infirmary of Sun looking through the tiny drawers containing their medicines then locking the cabinet after taking a small patch.

"It was the day you rescued us," he said.

Spin could see from the time stamp that it was within an hour after she told her she was on Cetrimemodel. "Keep this to yourself, thank you for telling me. I'll be aboard soon."

"Listen, if it comes to loyalty, or a question of rights, I'm with you on both counts. You saved me, not her, you, and she had no right to tamper."

"Thank you, Leland," Spin said, closing the connection. Her trust in Sun evaporated, burned away by a surge of hate that had her hands balled into fists and her eyes squeezed shut. A long education in self-control kept her from kicking and punching everything in front of her, and she breathed deeply, slowly until anger didn't blur her vision and muddy her thoughts. It was suppressed, to emerge another time. "She couldn't have meant to do it," Spin said to herself.

"Spin?" Nigel asked through the door.

"Come in," she replied. It wasn't Sun's intention to shorten her life, but she did, and it was all because she had to control what was going on around her, Spin included. She couldn't just let the drugs work their own way through her system, or have a conversation about ending the effects early. No, she had to sneak a counter-dose on the sly, Sun had to get her way. "I'm sorry, Nigel, I needed a minute."

"What's up?" he asked, sitting in the pilot's seat and turning towards her.

She looked at him as though seeing him for the first time, assuming nothing and inspecting. He really was concerned, it was all over his body language, his long face was deeply etched with it. He still had a little of that adolescent awkwardness tall people had even though he was twenty-three. Nigel and his friends were always kind to her, none of them had ever done anything to make her distrust them. She trusted Boro more than Sun, more than anyone, and Nigel was the one who introduced them. "I can trust you, can't I?"

"Yes," Nigel said without a split second's hesitation. "I can trust you too, right?" he asked, playing it up as though he was joining a conversation between two conspirators. His attempt at conversational play withered quickly, he could see how serious she was.

"If I can't trust you, then I'm alone," Spin said, aware that it would make a deep impression on Nigel. "I can't trust Sun, she's acting like I'm a child in her care, and it's backfired. I was going to help her, help everyone find a place before I died, now, with what she's done to me, I don't know if I can even look at her."

"What did she do?" Nigel asked. He was wide-eyed, concerned, and ready to become very angry with Sun.

"She saw how detached I was while I was on Cetrimemodel I guess, and without checking for adverse effects, or whether or not there was a genetic component to it, she touched me with a counter drug. All limited edition dolls die young, and I had about eleven months left, maybe more, but now, thanks to a safe-guard against genetic tampering that she activated, it's down to three."

"What?" Nigel asked. "She didn't mean to do it, but," he stammered. "Three months."

"It doesn't matter that she didn't mean to. Sun tampered with me, thinking I couldn't make my own decision about what I put into my system, taking charge like she always does. Now I only have time to help you and the few people I care about, or I have to chase a ghost of a chance that I might find a cure."

"Find the cure," Nigel said. "I'll do whatever you need, I'll go with you anywhere to get that done."

"Geist," Spin said. "The place I was made is there."

Nigel laughed and nodded. "It couldn't have been Paradiso or Sky Heaven. Well, we're going to Geist. You, me and Della and Mirra for sure. I bet you could get the Governor to help out somehow, and even Sun. I know she loves you like a daughter, it was a mistake."

"But if she won't trust me to make decisions for myself, there's no way she'll go along with what we have to do to get to Geist and get into the plant. This depends on a lot of information that's just alien to anyone who hasn't been inside the Countess' organization, anyone who doesn't know that corporate world."

"What if she gets control of the Cool Angel?"

"Today is revenge day, and I'm going to ruin Captain White, but the only way I can do that involves a risk that could burn her, it could burn me with the rest of the crew. I know why White betrayed Sun, Boro and me, and the secret we were keeping will get him killed. It'll either make the vote, or get us kicked off the ship for good."

"He did something before we were fucked over?" Nigel asked. "Boro didn't tell me about anything that would get the Captain spaced, you've gotta share."

"I'll do better than that, I'll show you," Spin said. "Let's get to the Exchange."

SIXTEEN

The blacked out faceplate on Aldo's helmet was the only thing that hid his disgust at what he had to watch early that morning. Before the sun broke the horizon, he and his partner, Corrine, escorted Master Kort to the main slave quarters. The horseshoe shaped housing complex was three stories tall, and was usually two thirds empty, but everyone had been called back from the factories, from the mines and the gentler service areas in the estate. The majority of the guards on and around the estate were called in as well, a hundred and forty-seven, all armoured and armed, were in attendance to make sure everything went smoothly.

Guards that Aldo didn't envy, and few of whom he knew, were tasked with bringing the slaves to the main courtyard in the middle of the complex. The first four groups didn't know what was going on until they saw the gun-like tagger that bonded a thin black strip bearing a code, a microns thick sealed poison layer and an equally small tracker to their skin.

Before they were on the honour system, if they tried to escape, they would be brought back, punished, implanted with a tag and sent back to work. Now they all had a black code that wound around their necks, and no chance of escape. The occasional slave would get free before, and a loss of less than one percent was acceptable, but that wouldn't be possible. The loss would be reflected in how many died by breaking their work and rest perimeters.

Master Kort watched as slaves were branded, unmoved by tears, by the ones who tried to run at the last moment. "Please, mistakes happen, these things kill innocent people. We know how dangerous it is out there, no one in my family has ever run," one woman pleaded, Thena, a respected person among the slaves. She shielded her nine-year-old daughter, Bea, from the end of the line. "You know us."

At Kort's small nod a pair of guards pulled Bea from her mother's arms and held her while the black strip was punched onto her by the printing gun. Her daughter returned to her, wailing, and Thena allowed them to tag her without resistance. "See? Mommy's getting one too, it's all right," she told her daughter. Thena was a good actress, she was able to hide whatever anger or sadness she had for her child's benefit, but it was a lie. What Master Kort was doing would be remembered by thousands of slaves, and Aldo was sure it would come back to haunt them somehow.

"They brought it on themselves," Corrine said. "If just one of them got in Aspen and Larken's way when they ran, none of this would be happening. They were treated like royalty here; it couldn't have taken much to convince them that running was wrong. I don't even understand why they left."

Aldo only nodded, remembering the presentation the Countess gave with crystal clarity. If he was told he would be breeding stock, forced to watch his children be sold, he would have done anything to change his fate, whether it meant running or jumping off the nearest balcony.

"Right?" Corrine pressed.

"Some people can't see the light while they're standing in it," he replied. It was something his grandfather said to him before the fall. Before a virus infected bulk loader bot crushed him to death.

"Captain, you will make sure that every slave in our inventory is tagged today. Any who leave the perimeter will be executed, and your pay will be docked for the loss. Do you understand?"

Captain Okan, who had a light green cape added to his armour so everyone knew who he was at a glance, turned to face Master Kort. "We will be finished by sundown."

Knowing him, they would be, and Aldo would be surprised if a single slave made it outside the perimeter. "Enough of this chore," Master Kort said as he turned away from the mournful lines. "The brand doesn't even cause pain, but these people act like we're using a hot brand." He stalked to a waiting hover car, with Aldo and Corrine close behind. He sat beside the driver, and they sat behind. "To the Shuttered House," Kort said.

Aldo was once amazed at the expansiveness of the green and blue estate. There were three palaces, the main one with its tall towers being the centrepiece. All of it existed under a blue energy shield that allowed things to leave, but not to enter. It served to mark the perimeter of the main living and leisure areas as well, and from where they moved across the broad lawn between the servant and utility buildings, he couldn't see the edge of it. It once seemed endless, but it started to feel like it was shrinking to him, even though he knew they had recently added a kilometre.

The mines on the planet and in the asteroids in orbit were secondary perimeters, staked so the slaves knew how far they could roam while working. Before they would be retrieved, now the toxin hidden against their necks would pass into their systems through the skin and kill them in minutes. Aldo knew the method of control from seeing how other masters controlled their slaves. He used to take pride in the fact that the Countess didn't employ those methods. Some efforts were even made to keep their slaves happy, but now that new enforcement methods were in place, he wondered how much longer they would have good medicine, good food, and good lodgings.

They arrived at the Shuttered House, a private prison disguised as a two story house. It was as well decorated as any other part of the estate, with trimmed square shrubbery, white finishing trim on the quartz brick, and a two story surrounding deck with guards on watch. They opened the double doors at Master Kort's approach and entered the modest foyer. There was only room for six people to stand, and the floor was solid marble, but the false front ended in that room. Through one more pair of secure doors there was a lift leading up and down to private cells and other areas of foul business.

They took the lift down, its metal walls polished so well that Aldo could see his reflection in it. The dark armour always made him look like some kind of humanoid insect, and the face-plate made all the guards look the same other than their height, and in some cases, their sex.

The doors opened and they followed Master Kort to the room at the end of the hall in the first subfloor. A waiting guard opened the door. "Good thing I'm used to waking up early," said the prisoner inside, who was strapped into a reclined chair made of self-sterilizing plastic. "I don't exactly know the day cycle of this planet yet, but it felt early."

"Talkative today, Boro?" Kort asked.

The captive looked older than most of the people Aldo had known in his life. Most people didn't allow themselves to physically age past thirty, paying for expensive medication that kept them rejuvenating at a nice rate, or stopped their apparent aging altogether in their twenties. Boro looked like he was in his mid-thirties, and if his file was correct, he actually was. Even still, he was a thickly built man, strong enough to manhandle two guards on each arm at the same time. Last time he decided to fight, it took the whole crowd at the Shuttered House to subdue him, and he was laughing as they brutally pinned him to the ground. A brawl was his idea of fun, and the only cybernetic part he had was a magnetic emitter in the bone of his middle finger, used to unscrew stubborn bolts and recover metallic objects.

"All I have are your visits, they won't let me have so much as a radio," Boro replied with a wry grin. He was relaxed, and spoke in low tones. Aldo would never admit it, but he liked the man. "Lots of time to think. That reminds me, I was wondering; since you serve a Countess, are there really still Kings in more than name? Did some dukes and duchesses survive all those murdering machines?"

"My Lady barely survived, but yes, there are many members of royal houses, though few used their titles before the

Fall. Now they're making a comeback, it makes it easier to put people in their places."

"Like she's the Countess and you're her official man-whore?" Boro laughed.

Aldo watched Master Kort flinch at the jibe, his hand tightened into a fist. Surprisingly, he exhaled and unclenched, shaking his hand as though to loosen his fingers. "I think it's time to get to work. How about answering my questions?"

"I told you everything I know," Boro said, shrugging but still in good humour. "Regular ports the Cool Angel visits, places Aspen liked, where we found her, and all the other info you were after. There's no point to any of it, why would they go back to anywhere familiar when they know you're looking?"

"Our early checks have reported no sign of them," Kort said. "But they couldn't have gotten far. Where would she hide? Never mind all the places you know she's been, what would she look for in a new hiding place? What kind of plan could she have?"

"Hey, I was just getting to know her," Boro said.

Kort activated a holoprojector and an image of Boro and Aspen dancing closely together, very closely, appeared in front of him. "She doesn't let people she barely knows that close."

Boro's expression softened, he looked the image over as though he was trying to commit it to memory. "Better days," he muttered. "We talked, we joked around for months. That one's wiser than her years, a lot of layers to her. I think I only just started to know her."

"All right," Kort said, deactivating the image. He summoned a control hologram beside the chair and activated a control hovering over Boro's right arm. Boro immediately began screaming, his hand gripping the chair arm, the rest of his body tensing. Master Kort deactivated the control when Boro ran out of breath. "That was the chair sending false signals across the nerves in your arm. That sensation was the feeling of your arm burning. Just the skin, mind you, just the part that would feel it, because if I was really burning you, the pain would lessen as those nerves were cooked. Now, where do you think she'd go? We know she has money, it disappeared into the Interplanetary Credit Exchange shortly after she was paid. We know she has a fast ship, she stole one, and Larken is an excellent pilot, so any unmonitored port would be open to them."

"They'd stay away from law," Boro said, panting. "The best way to do that is to find the places that were poor even before the Fall, places that would recover quick because there weren't as many AI's around to screw it all up."

"You're not telling me anything new," Master Kort said. "I'm going to access the major nerve bundles in your legs now."

"I told you, if this Larken is as smart as Aspen, then they're hiding better than I could. I wouldn't be able to find them."

"Not good enough," Kort said, selecting an image of feet and shins being crushed then activating it.

At first Boro writhed in silence, but as the machine simulated the slow crushing of all the bones in his feet and legs, the seal of his lips broke, and the room was filled with howls that made Aldo cringe. He could see his counterpart was cringing as well, and she was anything but squeamish.

Boro passed out as the counter on the holographic display passed seventy-three seconds. Kort stopped the stimulation and pressed another control that sent a pulse of some kind that forced Boro to become fully alert again, gasping for air. "You are still keeping something from me," Kort said. "I have all day, and this is a new toy. We've only scratched the surface of what it can do."

"I'm telling you that's everything," Boro said as he fought to catch his breath. "I've given you history, my best guesses, my gambling guesses, there's no more to tell."

"The sales representative told me to use this one," Master Kort said, bringing the image of a long barbed worm up in front of Boro. "It's a parasite that has been found in fruit on Yirist, they call it the Oetni. It translates as gut climber. I was told that an enterprising doctor recorded all the sensations this fellow creates when it travels through the digestive system, growing exponentially until it reaches the end of the small intestine. That's not very uncomfortable, but you see these barbs?" He pointed at the flexing barbs along the length of the worm's body. "The worm turns around once it realizes it's about to exit the small intestine, and digs in. Something about how it does that, and how it positions itself forces the bowels to flex, and try to pass it, which only makes the pain worse, only makes the tearing worse."

"You son of a bitch, I told you everything. I betrayed trust for you, you've got to see I've got nothing left."

"Let's start this playback just as the worm is turning and starting to fight," Master Kort said. "They provided scans to go along with the nervous system playback so you can watch what the worm would be doing inside you if it were real." He activated the simulation, and Aldo desperately wanted to look away from the meter-long worm as it twitched away from the end of the small intestine interior and turned around, struggling to climb back up. Boro closed his eyes, ground his teeth and began to sweat.

"Now the contest begins, the war between the worm and the patient's intestine," Kort said as the worm's barbs dug in. "I forgot to mention that it took over four hours and twenty minutes for this patient to die."

Boro didn't scream for nearly an hour, but after he started, he did not stop unless it was to catch a quick breath. His body shook, sweat dripped from him, and two hours in his bowels released. Somehow he did not pass out, but suffered for the duration of the simulation. Master Kort watched for the entire time, not goading, but observing the recreated scan and the reaction of his captive.

"It was only a simulation," he said as the playback stopped tricking Boro's nervous system. "I'm going to find something to eat, then we'll see what else is in the database."

"Aspen will want revenge on White, Captain White," Boro said. "Anyone would. Follow him, watch where his money goes."

"Why would I watch his money?" Kort said, leaning forward with interest.

"She set up a system of accounts for him to launder money, to turn his take from bullion to guaranteed credit."

"What do you mean, guaranteed credit?" Kort said. "How will this help me find her?"

"Don't you royal types know anything?" Boro asked.

Kort's hand moved towards the glowing red holographic control.

"Wait! Wait! Okay, Aspen created a bunch of accounts with

non-human banks who don't care where the money comes from, I think it was the Sti-Uls, the Nafalli Changers, and the ReMire Exchange. There were others, I'm sure. Once they shift it around, it's too hard for any human bank to get access to transfer records, to track the money. Then, it goes to a more legitimate alien account that will allow her to buy guaranteed credit with ICE."

"The Interplanetary Credit Exchange," Kort said.

"Right, but this isn't normal credit, it's backed by real money, that's why it's called guaranteed credit and it's considered high priority, spendable practically anywhere there's an Exchange. Really good for buying more bullion, like plat or UCA credit. Even better, the crew would think it's just normal credit, so he can spend as much as he wants and it'll only look like he's going further into debt when it's really all pre-paid. If she wants revenge on him, she won't go after him directly, she'll take the money she helped him hide."

"If there's any left."

"Captain White is hiding hundreds of millions from his crew, something she didn't know, but I did. Me and his First Officer, and probably Sun, one of his Lieutenants. That's probably why he gave us leave together, not just to sell Aspen out, but to get rid of everyone who knew except for his right hand man."

"I'm starting to like this Captain," Kort said. "This is something. This is something we can follow. Thank you, we'll catch her with this." He turned to Aldo. "Inform the Broadsword that we'll be under way in two hours. Contact the UCA and get the location of the Cool Angel from them, specifically request the location of Captain White as well."

"Yes, Sir," Aldo replied.

"Corrine, supervise the transportation of our guest here. I'm taking him and his special chair with us in case he's still holding back."

"You're a rare kind of asshole, Mister Kort," Boro said.

"That's Master, to you," Kort replied.

For a moment the pair locked gazes, both stern, calm and steady. Aldo was sure Kort would hit a button that would send Boro on another painful journey, but he turned and left instead.

SEVENTEEN

"I can't believe you know where all his money is," Nigel said. He listened quietly as Spin told him what she'd done for Captain White. There was no sign that he doubted any of it.

"She knew I could turn stolen funds into legitimate looking money, it's something that Larken and I used to do for the Countess' more questionable gains when we got older. Boro knew about it, Sun knew about it. Other Lieutenants probably knew too, but I only set up accounts for the Captain and Sun. Boro let the Captain legitimize his pay for him when the money was marked."

"The longer I'm away from the Cool Angel, the more I hear, the more amazed I am that anyone trusted Captain White," Nigel said. "I need payback on that waste of air."

"This is how we get it; I take all his money. It's something Boro knew I could do, he even warned me to stop helping White as soon as I could so the Captain couldn't use me as some kind of scapegoat. He said he liked having me around too much to watch me going out an airlock because I took the blame for some failed scheme."

"He more than liked having you around," Nigel said quietly as he piloted the ship into the secure zone of the new Exo-Terran Commerce Centre. They had been in a holding pattern for nearly three hours, it was the busiest port on the planet, and the most well-armed. The private guards manned defence turrets that idly scanned the skies for threats. Their navigational network looked as well organized as the old systems that were run by artificial intelligences before they were driven mad by the virus. "When I saw you two getting close, it was like watching two of my favourite things combined. Like ice cream and pudding, or macaroni and cheese. I think I'm a little hungry. Anyway, you guys seemed right together."

"He was the best of us. We'll do something for him, have a wake when we set up on a ship, a defensible ship," Spin said. She could see that he was still torn up about Boro, that would last for months, years. Boro wasn't as well loved as Larken was to her, but she felt his absence much more often than she would have expected. It was hard to think of him, grief and guilt pulled her down when she thought about him too much.

"For him and Trevor. We'll get spun on the best stuff we can find and sing some of those Irish songs Boro used to teach us," Nigel said. He set the small ship down in the centre of their small secure bay. He locked the controls. "God, I miss him."

Spin wrapped her arms around him from behind and cradled his head against her chest. "I wish he was here too."

"My whole family is gone, Spin," he whispered through tears.

"I'll stay with you," she replied, kissing the top of his head and stroking his hair.

He composed himself faster than she expected. "Okay, Boro would tell us to move on, take all of White's money," he said, wiping his eyes.

"He would," Spin agreed, releasing him and picking up her jacket.

They left the ship and locked it behind, meeting a boxy collections robot on the way out of the simple fenced landing spot. Spin dropped a ten platinum strip on top of the droid and nodded at the accompanying guard. The spiked helm did not reveal the inhuman face behind, but it nodded, leading the way through the secure fencing. A series of squelches and hisses emitted from it, and her translator went to work. "Thank you for paying your balance up front. If your business with the Exchange is valuable enough, your docking fees will be refunded. You are allowed to carry any non-antimatter personal weaponry with you, but any non-self-defence violence will result in your termination. Theft, speaking against the Kobunt Government, public breeding, and destruction of property will also result in your termination. Do you understand?"

"I understand," Spin said.

"I understand," Nigel added, "but I've gotta ask; is public breeding really a problem you get here?"

"We were visited by a clutch of Zilliosh two weeks ago and they held their mass bonding ceremony here. We thought it would be a wedding, we were woefully incorrect. It took nine days to clean and disinfect the food court."

"Wow," Spin said. "Don't worry, we're not that close, and he has terrible luck finding bonding partners."

"It's true. It hurts, but it's true," Nigel agreed.

"I am sorry for your misfortune, please continue through the gate. May you have better luck in the future, just not here," the guard said with a bow.

Spin led the way through the gate and made sure that the security code to get back in was downloaded into her personal computer before the tall metal gates closed and latched. Without delay, she moved on towards a tall bunker down the grey street. Instead of hawkers, there were shops with bright signs lining the well-organized streets. The patrons kept to themselves, mostly in small groups, but the attitude was not overly subdued.

"A million questions," Nigel said. "But let's start with this place looking like a military base. All the shops are stuck between big bunkers and hardened structures."

"It probably was one before off worlders settled here. The military were hit hardest by the Holocaust Virus, when the artificial intelligences were infected and went nuts, the soldiers were already surrounded."

"Yeah, so the-"

Spin stopped him with a look. "So the glorious Kobunt Government sent people here to take control and tame this area."

"Ah, nice of them to to that." He only waited a block before another question came bubbling to the surface. "Why not do the banking remotely?"

"For the level of withdrawals I'm going to be making, and the account changes that'll be done, I need to be in the Exchange building this time. Bioscans have to confirm that I'm Captain White's wife," Spin said. "According to the accounts

I'm about to access. No one knows, it's sort of a back door I left open for myself. They're all joint accounts."

"And there's no way he could know?" Nigel asked.

"Unless he looked at the fine print while he was spending some of his money, which he probably didn't do since he had the reward for turning me in anyway, then, no, it's buried in the paperwork. All he sees when he accesses these online accounts is the name 'White', it doesn't specify how many people with that name are on the accounts opening record."

"You're a genius. An evil one, but definitely a genius," Nigel said. His head turned with a jerk. "There's a Spacerwares Arms and Defence here."

"Do you have a weapon?" Spin asked.

"A little zap popper, but my real guns are probably still on the Cool Angel somewhere, or someone ran off with them when they left the ship."

Spin handed him her remaining UCA slips and platinum. "Okay, get us a pair of serious weapons. Handguns that can break down shields and burn through armour. If there's anything left, spend it on personal shields we can hide."

"I know exactly what we need, if that's a real store, like still hooked up to their parent stores, then they'll have it."

"Remember, practical but deadly," Spin said, hoping he could hear her through his excitement. "I'll do the boring stuff, the Exchange is right there."

"In that bunker?" He asked, nodding at the bunker half a block away. The heavy polished double doors beckoned.

"Yes, and just wait for me outside. They might not like you walking in with whatever you buy."

"True. Thank you, Spin." He hugged her and ran towards the brightly lit storefront. He didn't even notice the regular Spacerwares outlet right beside it.

"No grenades!" she shouted after him as an afterthought.

When she entered the bank the scanners flashed at her, and a disembodied voice said; "Welcome, Aspen White." Arrows on the floor directed her across the glassy black surface to a kiosk that was just as clean, and just as dark. A door closed behind her and the face of a gorgeous man appeared holographically only centimetres away from her nose. His blue eyes studied her, his smile was meant to disarm her, but she was firm in her purpose. "Access primary accounts and the accounts listed under the name Larken White." When she hid that name in the paper-work, Larken, she believed he had been dead for months. She thought it would be one of her last tributes to him.

The hologram was replaced with something much prettier to her in that moment, the records for five bank accounts, none of which were with human banking systems. Captain White had four hundred ninety-six million, three hundred seventy thousand, four hundred twenty-three International Currency Exchange Credits left. ICE, the Interplanetary Currency Exchange, based its currency on the value of platinum, which had been relatively steady for centuries. In United Core Authority credits it was worth half. "So much more money than you should have, Captain. There's no way you made that without ripping the crew off. If turning me in for a bounty wasn't bad enough, skimming off the top of everyone's share will finish you off."

She dug a little deeper into the deposits and payments and

discovered that the repairs and refitting on the Cool Angel only cost him five million in UCA, and he was paid twenty-five million for betraying her. He didn't earn anything for the other crewmembers he betrayed. The bounty payment was clearly marked. "I'll take that," she said to herself as she motioned for that amount to be moved into her own accounts, where it would be filtered through several non-human banks so no one could recover it. She was standing in the exchange, so she watched the pre-scripted money laundering happen in front of her, and when it was finished the amount was down sixty thousand UCA thanks to fees, but it was hers. "Teller," she said, addressing the supervised automated system built into the kiosk.

"Yes, Aspen?"

"Please move all of our funds to the new account I'm giving you, then divide them evenly amongst the list of people I'm about to send you. Lock the funds behind the password I'm setting now," Spin watched as the rest of Captain White's funds were drained and sent to his crewmembers. When the account reached zero, she couldn't help but giggle. "Now close all of the White accounts please." Her personal shadow account, set up with her DNA but under a name that was just a long number, was separate from the accounts she set up for Captain White.

"Are you sure?" asked the teller's voice from above. "That act is irreversible."

"Yes." Spin said. "I'm sure." The account reports disappeared one by one until only her shadow account remained. "Now, switch identities to Spin Seven and confirm with a scan." The scanner flashed.

"Identity confirmed, hello Spin Seven," replied the Teller's voice. Her account transaction appeared and she was delighted to see all the money she earned by ransoming Dexter and Tilly Rinnel. The amount made her grin. After dozens of banks charged fees for opening and closing accounts while transferring the money, she was left with seventy million, twenty-one UCA credits. "I have the money, now I need people I can trust," she said to herself. With a few quick transfers she made the currency available to herself under a fresh identity that could only be activated using a deep biometric scan. The kind of scan her wrist computer could do on her from where it was imbedded in her skin. "I want twelve million in UCA credits delivered to my ship."

"Is this your ship?" asked the Teller, showing her a hologram of their new ship and the landing area.

"It is," she replied. "Can I request that a guarded delivery be made elsewhere later?"

"Yes, for a fee of five hundred UCA credits. We will guarantee its safe delivery anywhere in the solar system."

"That's fair. Thank you. Please give me twenty thousand UCA credits in large denominations and one thousand in pips and small coin. Then shut down and disallow any access to my account unless I scan in."

"Thank you for doing business with the Interplanetary Currency Exchange, enjoy long life," the teller said as a tray emerged from the wall, laden with strips of platinum that glittered with industrial diamond dust that had been coded to foil counterfeiting. They reflected light in different colours depending on their denominations. The smaller amounts were in slim strips and small round pips that were too small to be considered coins. She stashed her money away in the smaller pockets inside the tops of her boots, and in her jacket pockets so they didn't jingle when she moved. "Captain White should notice that he's dirt poor any second now," she muttered with a grin as the doors to the kiosk opened.

EIGHTEEN

"Please, help me," Dorian said into his communicator using the voice of Keith Daniels, the first mate of the Cool Angel. "Lieutenant Sun is here, and she used her cyborg to kidnap me. They're going to kill me." He grinned and waited for a response.

"Keith, it's Gordon, we're coming for you, man! Where are you?"

"I'm pinging you my coordinates right now, I've gotta go, someone's coming," Dorian pinged the location of the Fleet Feather and cut the signal. From his perch in the rafters of the large hangar holding the Cool Angel he waited and watched.

Getting away from the Fleet Feather was easy. After he delivered Keith to the infirmary everyone was distracted, and if anyone saw him leave the ship, they didn't say anything to stop him or give chase. Deciding on how to distract the small loading crew aboard the Cool Angel was another thing entirely. He could have stormed the rear of the ship, catching them with the ramp open and slaughtering the lot of them. He could have hacked into one of the secondary hatches, but there was no power throughout most of the ship, so getting it open would have been difficult and loud because he'd still have to pull it open manually. Stowing away in one of the supply crates was a good idea, but there was always the chance that he would have to wait until the crew left the cargo compartment, and that could take hours.

After nearly an hour and a half of pondering his options and watching the behaviour of the loading crew, he came to a decision. He would have to send trouble towards the Fleet Feather. When he checked on Nigel's location and found that he was on the other side of the planet, far from harm, he decided he could live with the consequences.

He almost giggled to himself as he watched the entire loading crew, some still wearing strength exoframes, storm out of the ship's main ramp. Nine in all, they loaded into an old troop transport, armed and ready for a fight then sped out of the hangar. Dorian started a scan of the area far beneath him and lit one of his last Dice cigars. The results passed through his mind as he puffed at it and felt the tingle that always preceded the mad rush. The main aft loading ramp was still open, and his scans said there was still someone there.

He took one long puff on the cigar, his head swimming with glorious intense sensation. The world around him seemed to slow down, and when he looked at the heat bloom of the last crewman by the loading ramp, he could make out new details. The head, the shoulders, the beating of his fragile human heart. "Have to stay clear for this one," Dorian muttered to himself, letting the cigar drop from his mouth. It was already half gone.

Faster than the cigar fell, he swept down from his perch and landed in front of the crewman. It wasn't anyone he recognized from his time on the Cool Angel. He snatched the man's head in his hands. "Where is Captain White?"

"His cabin," the crewman replied, stunned. "He freaked out a few minutes ago," he said, struggling to free himself futilely.

Dorian tightened his grip, sure he was bruising the thin skin covering the man's skull. "You are going to run now, and if you warn anyone that I'm here, I will track you down and tear you into scraps. Do you understand?" He didn't wait for an answer, letting go instead.

The crewman ran towards the ship at first, then seemed to come to his senses and sprinted away from the loading door, towards the nearest hangar exit. Dorian moved as fast as he could through the main loading door, closed it behind him, and then pushed on at a dead run through the corridors. He couldn't help but recall his time aboard with Boro, Trevor, Nigel and the rest of the crew. It seemed like the best time of his life as he learned how the ship worked, spent time lazing around with his oldest friends, and felt as though he was surrounded by a growing family.

It was all overshadowed by Captain White's inflexible response to the accusation that he wasn't paying the crew fairly. Dorian did the math after they were all paid for a bank robbery, and from what he saw when they cracked the vault open, it looked like their share was short by half. Accusing the Captain directly was a mistake. Once he made the accusation, offers to take it back were worthless, and the only mercy White granted was the choice of which nearby port he would be left on. He told his friends to stay aboard the Cool Angel, it was one of the best ships in the region, but he warned them to keep a watchful eye. They were hesitant, but remained, mostly because Boro gave his word to Captain White that they'd remain until the end of the year. Then, they would have enough for their own ship, and pick him up no matter where he was.

He was crushed between two ships, assumed dead by most before then. The cargo section of the ship was behind him in less than a minute. He managed to go around two crewmembers who were stowing spare parts, and was sure he wasn't noticed. Dorian's path through the four hundred fifty-metre-long ship took him up three decks through emergency crawl ways, forward past the galley where he attended more birthday parties and celebrations than he could count, then up two more access shafts and he emerged at the rear of the command deck.

There were three people there, his thermal imaging system saw them through the walls. He quietly moved around the corner, eager to meet the first in the middle of the only four way crossing of corridors and came face to face with Burt Franco, the Tactical Officer for the Cool Angel. Dorian barely had occasion to speak to him while he was aboard, but he remembered the short, skinny man well. He was still human, but had an appetite for performance enhancing drugs that made Dorian's look tame. "Holy hell, what are you?" he said as he turned towards him at the worst possible moment and stepped backwards with impressive alacrity.

"Just here to pay the Captain a visit," Dorian said, reaching for him as quickly as he could. He caught the man by the wrist and yanked him closer. "I hear he's resting in his cabin?"

"Bridge," Burt said, somehow slipping his grip then running down a narrow corridor leading aft. "You'll find him on the bridge."

Dorian realized that he was still holding Burt's wrist. Sometime since he was left behind, the Officer had at least one of his forearms replaced with a detachable model. The thought that he was willing to shed a limb and leave it behind to escape amused him, so he dropped it and decided not to pursue. "Bet I'll find you useful." The run to the bridge was quick, and he was able to push right past two crewmembers working behind it. The armoured doors to the control centre of the ship were closed, but Dorian knew how they were put together. He used his cutter to slice the bolts hidden under the main armour sheeting protecting the door, then pulled the double doors apart. "Captain White!"

He ducked and dove to the left, behind one of the older, sturdier consoles at the rear of the bridge as bolts of energy sizzled past his head. "I almost got off this fucking planet without running into any of you," Captain White said.

He was instantly recognizable since he dressed to suit his name. A long armoured white coat, a mane of white hair, and painted white cutter pistol made him instantly recognizable. To Dorian, it made him look fancy and weak. "I'm just here for the ship," Dorian said. "Quino would like to see you dead, but he really wants the Angel."

"Like explaining yourself will make this a transaction instead of an act of piracy? You already have all my money, you could buy four Cool Angels with that take alone."

"I have no idea what you're talking about, White. Hand over your command codes, and I let you walk." Several shots burst against the opposite side of the console Dorian hid behind. "That's a no?" he watched the Captain begin moving towards the port side exit through his scanners. He was pinned down, but if he didn't do something, the Captain would escape.

Dorian burst into a run around the rear of the bridge towards Captain White, staying as low as he could, and activated a personal shield. Captain White fired while he rushed for the exit, making his shots unsteady. Only one streak of energy struck Dorian's shield. The whine of the small device told him it was close to burning out.

Dorian lurched towards Captain White as he rounded the last console and caught him as another shot struck the shield. The emitter overloaded with a small pop. He batted the cutter pistol out of the Captain's hand and gripped him by the throat. "The command codes, and I don't start breaking bones."

"My people will be here soon, you'd best run if you don't want to get parted out for spare limbs," Captain White said.

Dorian's scanner told him otherwise. The few people left on the command deck were leaving in a hurry. "I don't know what you've been doing, Captain, but no one's coming, no one wants to save you. I might be your best friend right now, or at least the most honest one you have. Give me the command codes and you have my word, I won't take your life."

"You don't hold that Captain's post as long as I have without making important friends, boy." To Dorian's surprise, his visual and main auditory sensors went dead. His damage system told him that he'd suffered serious damage, and most of his head was gone. The world slipped sideways and he fell to the floor. "Or without learning a few tricks," Captain White said. He moved to the command seat and began the initialization sequence for the ship. Heat and secondary audio sensors told Dorian that the whole ship was warming up. There were indeed two people coming up to the command deck and they were moving fast.

His secondary systems finished taking over for the damaged and missing components that were housed in his machine skull, and he quietly stood. Dorian crept up on the Captain from behind, and was one step away when White turned around and blasted him in the hip. It took three attempts for him to snatch the hand White held the small holdout blaster in, each attempt faster than the last. With hand and blaster in his grasp, he squeezed until the two were crushed together in shreds of metal, bone and flesh. "You think I'd keep my brain box in my head? Stop thinking like a human, Captain. Give me your command codes and you can keep your other hand." He said using his secondary speaker, it was a scratchy, loud voice that cut through Captain White's screams.

With his free hand, White pulled the collar of his fine tunic down to reveal a necklace shaped like a three pointed star. "In the data chip!"

Dorian got his hand around it and was about to duck when several bolts of energy tore through his armoured jacket then into his cyborg body. His right hip joint failed, followed by the main stabilizer system in his stomach, then the protective case housing the synthetic organs that fed his brain everything it needed reported a critical failure. "You die today, White." He said as he felt the emergency stasis drugs that may save his grey matter begin to put him to sleep. "Someone will finish this."

As his sensors began to go dark, he watched Captain White turn towards perhaps the last faithful crewmembers he had. "We fall back to the Hexer."

NINETEEN

"I'm broke," Nigel told Spin happily as the complimentary shuttle dropped them off at their Long Runner. He carried a lightly armoured case with him, the purchases he wanted to show her as soon as they got to their small ship.

The delivery of her cash was already there, waiting in their landing space. "Your docking fees, refunded as promised." A guard said as he handed her the coinage. "Thank you for doing business with us. Would you like us to load your cargo onto the shuttle?"

"Thank you, we'll open it up for you," Spin said.

Nigel opened the Long Runner's main hatch, eying the heavily armoured transport that had landed beside their ship. There were two heavy turrets on top, and the main cabin had enough room for six large soldiers. From a small segment between the troop carrier portion at the rear and the cockpit in the front, a pair of robots with thin appendages emerged carrying her credit cases. They made them look light, bearing one each, but Spin knew that she would barely be able to lift one on her own, it would take Nigel and her to carry those for more than a few metres at a time. "Is that all money?" Nigel asked in a whisper as they moved towards the Long Runner.

Spin nodded and directed the short robots to a panel in the floor that would have enough cargo space for all three cases. "You're not broke, either. I'm going to do something now, and I need you to try not to react."

"What?"

Spin unlocked his portion of the money Captain White had hidden, and she watched as he checked the computer display that he had tattooed on the palm of his hand. Nigel's shock at seeing over six million real credits in his account was comical, watching him try to hide his grin and amazement was even better. "Why are you paying me enough to buy my own combat ship?" he said under his breath.

"Oh, that's not from me," Spin said as she watched the third credit case get carried to their Long Runner. "That's from Captain White. You remember how he used to go on about spending every last pip on his ship, leaving a pittance for himself while the crew got paid?"

"I remember, he used to say 'pittance' a lot, you couldn't do a good imitation without it," Nigel replied. "Wait, this is from him? He was hiding this? Why give it all to me?"

"That's your share, I sent the whole crew their portions, but used a password to delay delivery," Spin replied. "I wanted you to get your share first so it wouldn't be a surprise when I give everyone else theirs at the vote."

"He's going to blame you, he'll put a bounty on your head," Nigel said.

"With what money? He doesn't even have hidden accounts anymore," Spin said. "He really should have had the patience to let me teach him how to hide his money, instead of telling me to do it for him."

"Being lazy can make you stupid," Nigel said. "Another Boro-ism. Guess it's true. So, those bots are loading more money than anyone aboard the Cool Angel has ever seen onto our little ship."

"Yes," Spin said. "If we didn't have slave marks on us, and we could spend it wherever we liked, we'd be wealthy."

"Is it all from White? I mean, I'm just wondering because I need to know how much he's losing."

"This is from ransoming Della and Mirra's old masters, so it's ill-gotten, but it's mine, and partially theirs."

"Wow, it makes my shopping trip look a little small."

"We're finished transferring the cargo," the guard said. "Would you like to scan it to make sure it's all there?"

Spin got aboard the shuttle and used the basic scanner built into her computer to scan the open cases of glittering currency. "It's all there, thank you," she called to the guard outside.

"You are welcome, we at the Interplanetary Currency Exchange wish you a long life and good journey."

"Thank you, good luck," Nigel said as he boarded the shuttle. He stopped dead in his tracks at the sight of the coins and rectangular slips of platinum in their cases. The fine diamond coating on the UCA credit slips glittered in the half-light while the regular platinum coins caught the half-light on their edges and star punched faces. "You know, you could buy a serious ship with all this money," he said. "Pay a crew for a while too."

"I know, but it wouldn't last under our names. The Core

Authority still has us marked as slaves, even if their records show we're still in the Estate's custody."

"Ah, right. The Estate?" he asked as he helped her close the cases and replace the deck plate over the small cargo compartment.

"Oh, I meant in the Countess' custody."

"Well, we could head towards British Alliance territory, they still don't allow slavery there," Nigel said. "If we got a wormhole generator for this thing, we could do it for sure. It would be cramped for a couple weeks, but possible."

"I know your head is spinning right now," Spin said, sitting down. "But this money doesn't change as much as you think it does. I still have things I need to do here, and I still can't trust more than a couple people, maybe, so I don't know where I'm going for sure next. With the money you have now you really could run, resettle somewhere where you'd be free, that would be safe, smart."

"Why do I get the feeling that I'd probably be going alone?" Nigel asked. "You wouldn't come with me if I did, would you."

"There are things I want to do in this sector," Spin said. "I wouldn't blame you if you wanted to start a new life somewhere safer though."

"No, I'll go where you're going. I owe you, and you've always been just, well, nice to me. No matter what I get up to, or whatever trouble I got in, you never judged me. You're right, that's more important than money. What would I do all alone in British space anyway?"

"Thank you, Nigel," Spin said, wondering if she'd have to send him off on his own anyway. Her future may be short, but it could get dangerous. She didn't want to lead him to his death, like she did with his friends and uncle. "What's in the case? What did you buy?"

"Well, it doesn't glitter or shine like your take," Nigel said, his smile returning. He opened the case to reveal two vicious looking holstered sidearms. "They're Raptor 9's." He took one from the case, drew the thickly barrelled weapon and decoupled the front half. "Without the forward section of the gun it's a powerful stunner that's legal practically anywhere. The discharge is adjustable, and it has seven thousand shots on the lowest setting, which is enough to stun the average sized human. It only has about three hundred fifty shots on the highest setting, but that's enough to stun a small family of Nafalli."

"Okay, looking good so far," Spin said, taking one of the holsters and slipping the straps through loops in her high boot.

"Okay, here's why this is one of the best weapons they had," Nigel said, snapping the front of the pistol on. "This is a particle emitter, and it changes the stun energy into a lethal bolt that, along with the accelerated particles, can cut through light hull plating with one or two shots. It's a little loud, but that's because of the accelerator." He handed the weapon to her and smiled. "With the power recycling technology in the weapon, you can get about three thousand shots out of it before replacing the battery cartridge. Fires at eleven rounds a second on full auto, and it can sustain that for thirty-five seconds before having to cool down."

There was a significant weight to the weapon, but it felt balanced, and good, powerful in her hand. "I'm usually not a gun person, but this is a beautiful weapon."

"They said it was one of the most reliable models they've

sold. A few customers there told me I couldn't go wrong either," he said, taking his own and strapping it on.

Spin set hers to single fire, and made sure the safety was on before slipping the whole assembled weapon into its holster and locking it in. "This is good, thank you."

"Oh, that's not all," he said. "I had enough left over to get us these Rank Three shield emitters. They're generic, but they'll protect you from physical or energy damage for a minute before running out of power, or a few hits before they burn out."

Spin had seen them before, a short tube that was thin enough to hide in clothing. She accepted one and stood so she could calibrate it by holding a tiny recessed button on the side of it. It blinked green and chirped twice to signal that it was finished measuring her shape, then she put it in an inside pocket.

"You've seen those before," Nigel said.

"Just from the boarding crew on the Cool Angel. Sun made sure I watched and learned about every part of how the Angel's crew worked. This was one of those things that the boarders who could afford them swore by."

"Yeah, they cost about as much as the guns. I always thought shielding was way overpriced," Nigel said.

"They still sell by the thousands, I'm sure," Spin said. "That's probably the problem."

"So, did I do all right?" Nigel asked.

"Really well," Spin replied. "Thank you. I knew you'd, wait, one sec, Mirra's calling. "

"Spin!" came Mirra's voice over her communicator. "The ship is under attack, there are a bunch of people trying to get in, they've got exoframes."

"Where's Dorian?"

"I don't know; Leland says he left the ship a while ago. Jorin tried to call him, but his comm isn't even on."

"Have you tried Sun?"

"She has privacy mode on, we left her a message."

"We're on our way," Spin replied.

TWENTY

From the turret in the Long Runner, Spin could see the section of the landing field reserved for the Fleet feather as it came into view. The metal walls of the so called secure space had been bent and torn open and a small group of people guarded the rear of the Fleet Feather while three more of them in exo-suits made to amplify their strength many times over were working on tearing through the hull at the aft of the ship.

The turret beeped cheerily and the small targeting screen turned green, indicating that the guns had a full charge. They were too far up to be noticed, but as soon as she opened fire she knew all attention would be on their lightly armed shuttle. "Still no word from Sun?" Nigel asked from the pilot's seat below.

"Nothing," Spin said, feeling even more trust for her mentor slipping away. "I'm going to start with warning shots."

"That's awfully nice of you, since they're about to get in there. They're working on an unarmoured interior cargo bay bulkhead."

Spin raked the ground between the five people guarding the rear of the ship, and they all ran for cover. The turret reported that it was already at low power, and needed four seconds to recharge. "I think we got ripped off on this ship."

"On the weapon systems, sure, I mentioned that to Sun. Everything else is great though," Nigel said.

Three of the workers from the Cool Angel began firing back, their small sidearms shouldn't have done much to their shields, but Spin saw a significant drain in defensive strength, and they began to recharge, adding five more seconds to the recharge time on her turret. "Unfortunately, the weapon systems are pretty important right now. This disappointment might get us killed."

"That bad?" Nigel asked.

"My turret is telling me that it needs another twenty-eight seconds to recharge now, it just keeps going up. Get some distance so everything can recharge, and see what you can do about re-routing power."

"Can't do that," Nigel said. "There's no control for diverting power. This is a glorified runabout," he replied as he began to guide the Long Runner into a course that would put them out of range.

A bald crewman in an exosuit emerged from the rear of the Fleet Feather brandishing a shard of metal torn from somewhere inside the ship and he hurled it at them like a javelin. Spin felt the shard penetrate the hull beneath her feet, and heard a change in the vessel's sound that was too drastic to be minor. "Nigel, are you okay?"

"Missed me, but hit our port thruster, the controls are trying to compensate, but it feels like they're fighting me too. I told you I'm not much of a pilot."

"No you didn't!" Spin said.

"Oh, maybe that was just in my head," Nigel said. "We're landing, by the way. Quickly."

"No, we're crashing," Spin said, bracing herself as she saw the ground, the sky, then the ground flash by her turret display. It chirped cheerfully, indicating that it was fully charged again as they rushed towards the ground. "Slow us down?"

"Trying," Nigel said through his teeth.

At the last second, the shuttle whirled violently, Spin heard the main thrusters fire harder than ever before and was thrown against one side of her seat. Another hard jostle followed less than a second behind. All was silent except for a polite voice that stated; "You have suffered a hard landing. Please return to a Pearson Dealership to have your Long Runner serviced."

"Saved it!" Nigel declared. "Are you okay?"

"Doing fine," Spin said, slipping out of the chair and dropping to the main deck behind the cockpit. She drew her new firearm and activated it. While she waited a moment for it to power on, she couldn't help but notice that he was right, he really did land their ship on its landing gear and, according to the simple display in the cockpit, they only sustained damage to their main port thruster and two struts under the ship. "How'd you manage that?"

"Trick with the thrusters, forced the ship to auto level by increasing throttle at the last second," Nigel said, powering his Raptor handgun on. It immediately came to life, unlike hers, which seemed to be taking its time. "What now?"

Spin was about to answer, but then the calm voice of a

woman began coming from her sidearm. "Thank you for purchasing a Raptor Nine, Revision Three sidearm from Diretech. This short tutorial is made to -"

"Skip tutorial," Spin said to her sidearm.

"I already went through all this," Nigel said.

"Skipping tutorial," the weapon replied. "Please pay close attention to these important advisories."

"Skip advisories!" Spin said.

"I'm sorry, we are legally obliged to share these important advisories concerning your purchase. Please pay attention."

"Seriously?" Spin asked as she peeked through the cockpit window and saw two men in exosuits and three others brandishing side arms approaching their ship.

"I did this with mine in the store," Nigel said.

Spin hit the button to open the rear hatch of the ship, and kicked the lowering mechanism, forcing the ramp to drop faster. She drew her other sidearm from inside her jacket and stepped outside firing at the nearest crewmember, who crumpled as she took two sizzling hits, one in the middle of her chest, the other in the shoulder. Before anyone could get a bead on her, Spin was behind the ship.

"Please ensure that the Raptor Nine is powered down before cleaning. It is important to clean your weapon before storage, after storage and every ten thousand rounds," the voice from her new sidearm droned. "Do not point your weapon at yourself for any reason. Looking directly at the firing mechanism while it is facing you should not be necessary when cleaning or using the weapon properly."

Spin waited for several shots to pass before leaning out the other side and scoring a direct hit on one of the exosuit clad crewmen. She cursed under her breath as she saw the woman she'd shot before taking cover behind a large waste bin, she seemed no worse for wear thanks to the protection of the crew suit she was wearing.

"Do not attempt to connect the Raptor Nine to another device with the intention of power sharing. The power cell inside can be used for other purposes, but the high powered systems inside your new weapon are not compatible with unrecognized components," the voice continued.

"Cover me," Nigel said. "I'm coming out!"

Spin ran to the other side of the ship and leaned out, firing as quickly as she could with her old sidearm. It didn't seem to do much against the basic protective jumpsuits the crew of the Cool Angel wore, and they were quickly learning that. Even still, Nigel came out firing his own Raptor sidearm, and Spin couldn't help but appreciate the weapon as it rapidly spat bright bolts of light that scarred the plastcrete covered ground and one of the exosuits. Nigel managed to join her on the other side of the ship without getting shot.

"Finally, we at Diretech hope you have a long and healthy life thanks to the defensive capabilities you've gained with your wise purchase. Thank you," the voice concluded. The weapon finished powering up and Spin re-holstered her light weapon, finally drawing the Raptor from where it had been speaking against her thigh.

"You're going to like that," Nigel said with a grin.

"Last warning!" Spin shouted. She took a deep breath as the sounds of laughter drifted from the other side of the shuttle. "We will shoot to kill."

"Come on out, baby!" said one of the crewmen on the other side of the ship. He punctuated his goad by rocking the shuttle.

Spin turned her new weapon up to its maximum setting. "This ship was brand new today," she muttered angrily. "Sure I could buy a fleet of them now, but I like this one."

"What are you going to do?" Nigel asked, looking a little frightened.

She activated her personal shield and ran from cover, they were ready, firing at her but not striking at first. She opened fire on the first crewman she saw, white-yellow light piercing the air between them at a rate so rapid that it almost looked like a steady stream. His suit did not protect him. Wherever the weapons' fire touched, it left molten, charred or flaming damage behind. Spin was able to hit a second crewman in the leg before diving behind the cover of a heavy storage crate. The creaking and popping of the metal on the other side told her that her enemies were firing at it, her cover would be gone before long.

The personal shield beeped a warning and began to heat up. She tossed it on the ground, where it sparked and steamed, surprised that it was burned out, she didn't notice that she'd taken any hits. The enemy fire shifted focus as Nigel took pot-shots from behind the Long Runner, several of which dug into a crewman wearing an exosuit.

"Grenade!" shouted another crewman wearing an exo-skeleton as he ran as fast as he could from the torn aft of the Fleet Feather. "It's a big one!"

Everyone else ran for cover, except for Spin, who took aim at the crewman who was trying to rock the Long Runner onto its side. When her aim was sure, she squeezed the trigger, ripping through him with more rounds than she could count in one second. He fell to the ground, bleeding and burning, missing his right arm.

A riot of music, confetti and novelty spray webbing erupted from the rear of the Fleet Feather, and Spin couldn't help but grin as she and Nigel stepped out from behind cover, their weapons pointed at the three remaining crewmembers from the Cool Angel.

"What the fuck was that?" asked one as he stared in disbelief at the colourful scene.

"It was a party bomb," Nigel chuckled from behind them. "Picked it up in a store I hit a while ago."

It couldn't have done any harm to a new-born baby at point blank range, but it was just as good as a big, fat grenade for the commotion it caused. The enemy crew were taking cover from it, exposing their backs to Spin and Nigel. "Drop your weapons, kick them over there," Spin ordered.

"What the hell, Terrance?" spat a long haired crewmember. "Grenade?"

"It was big, round, green and ticking! Someone must have painted it or something, then dropped it through the hole I made over my head," replied Terrance, the exoskeleton clad man they'd sent to the rear of the Fleet Feather to open the aft bulkhead.

"Take off the exo-frame," Nigel said. "Now."

"Why are you here?" Spin asked as the enemy crew took everything that could be considered a weapon off and she checked faces. She didn't recognize any of them.

"We got a message from the First Officer saying he got nabbed, and he was here," said Terrance.

"We're giving him medical treatment because he tried to

run when we spotted him," Spin said. "He's fine, we'll be bringing him back to the Angel in an hour or two when our medic clears him. Did you knock before trying to rip through the hull?"

"I just followed Gregor's lead," Terrance replied apologetically. "He said it was better to make a door and apologize later than to knock and get shot."

"Which one is Gregor?" Spin asked. Terrance pointed to the last man she killed, the one in the exosuit next to the shuttle, and she nodded. There was little left of his head, so no chance of revival. "Well, I hope this doesn't overwrite the good I'll be doing for your crew."

"Oh my God, what the hell did you do?" Nigel said as he got a look at the only working turret on the Fleet Feather, well, formerly working. The barrels had been bent and the rotary ball was part way out of its socket. "And what the?" he said, looking more closely at the rear of the ship where someone in an exosuit – most likely Terrance – punched fist sized holes through an interior bulkhead. "The Feather isn't even space worthy anymore! What were you doing back here? Trying to get in, or just being an asshole to whoever had to fix it later? Me! That's me! I have to fix this!" Nigel said, whirling towards Terrance and waggling his steaming weapon at him.

Terrance cringed half way to kneeling. "I'm sorry, man! I'm new to the Angel! Wanted to score points with the commander."

"Can I shoot him? It won't make the repairs go faster, but I'll feel better. Please, can I shoot him?" Nigel begged Spin.

"Is it safe?" the Governor asked in Spin's comm.

She laughed at Nigel and shook her head. "We'll get him to

help you, I'm sure the Angel can spare him." Spin answered her communicator. "It's safe. We've got it under control. Just wondering, who dropped the party bomb?"

"It was Della's idea. There wasn't much else we could do from here, but we thought a distraction was better than nothing, so we painted it and dropped it through a hole."

"It worked, good thinking," Spin said, laughing to herself.

TWENTY-ONE

There was no doubt about it, the firefight that happened next to the Fleet Feather was the loudest thing to happen on the whole continent. The continent that happened to have at least one contingent of United Core Authority ship hovering over it, or set down on it. Whatever was going to happen, it had to happen fast. Her inspection of the damage to the Fleet Feather took ten minutes with Nigel's help.

Inspecting their Long Runner took only a little longer, and to her it came down to one question; "Which one will take less time to repair?" she asked Nigel as he finished extracting the large shard of metal that had destroyed the main port thruster with Leland's help.

"This looks bad, and if we were still flying around, it would be," Nigel explained, nodding at the devastated thruster. "But almost all the damage was to that one component, and the Long Runner uses pretty standard parts. I've already contacted the dealer, and they have spares. We can get one delivered in ten minutes, and with this guy's help we can have this swapped out in about an hour. The Fleet Feather needs patching and I need to replace a main aft support that got torn up by some asshole in an Exo Suit."

Spin looked to the small parts shed where the three survivors were tightly bound. The bodies of the fallen were piled under a tarp, something that made Spin cringe, if she had more time they would have done something that showed a little more respect. "So, how long for that?" she asked.

"Eight hours if I rush it and have all the metal? I can source what I need from scrap, but that takes time too."

"There's life support for everyone if we're forced to take off in the Long Runner. Get it fixed up, and get us the modules that are missing."

"You mean the wormhole generator and the supercharger module?" Nigel asked.

"If the Supercharger module will help with the power reserve issue I had with the guns, then yes, both."

"It'll solve it, and extend the jump distance," Nigel said.

"That sounds expensive," Leland said.

"That's not a problem we have anymore," Spin said quietly. "Just hope we don't have to get out of here in this thing. The life support will take care of us, but it will be cramped."

"I haven't seen anything on the local 'net about the fight yet," Della said as she emerged from the Fleet Feather. "Do you think it'll get picked up?"

"Definitely," Spin replied. "There must be so many privately owned watcher bots drifting above us that it'll be posted from ten different angles before sundown."

"So we're runnin' then, soon?" she asked.

"I'm sorry, Della," Spin said. "You should get some essentials together in case we don't have time to repair the Feather."

"Oh," she looked at the Long Runner for a long moment. "A small bag," Della said. "I'll tell everyone else."

"Thank you," Spin said. She turned to Leland. "How is your patient doing?"

"Healing faster than expected, but I couldn't wake him up while we were under attack, otherwise that might have been cut short."

"I understand, don't worry about it."

"But that is going to be trouble," he said, nodding at the shed. "How bad?"

"We're about to find out," Spin said as she watched one of the Cool Angel's shuttles descend towards their landing area. With the shuttle that was already there from the attacking crew, the Long Runner, and the Fleet Feather, there would be almost no room left. The passenger hatch began opening before the shuttle touched down, and Spin decided that there would be no better time to send a big reveal to the Cool Angel crew. It wasn't the way she planned it, but she had a sinking feeling that she had to take care of her interests so the people who trusted her wouldn't be stranded or worse. As quickly as she could, Spin attached a message to the money she was holding for the Cool Angel crew. It said;

THIS WAS STOLEN *from you by Captain White and I am returning it to the crew of the Cool Angel. This is your share; I'm keeping the bounty he collected on me. Courtesy of, Spin.*

· · ·

SPIN ADDED the deposit records and entered the password that sent shares to everyone who was serving on the Cool Angel when she was captured. When she finished, Sun was setting her foot down on the black and grey plastcrete of the landing area. "What the hell is going on?" she asked. "Are you trying to take the Angel behind my back?"

The accusation took Aspen by surprise. Nothing she did, except for the redistribution of funds, looked to her like a play for the Cool Angel. "I have no idea what you're talking about."

Hugo, just as furious, led two crewmembers off the shuttle as they carried a heavily damaged torso with Dorian's long coat hanging off it. They threw it to the ground. "Leland!" Spin cried, and the medical technician was already running towards the corpse with Nigel right behind.

"He tried to kill Captain White for the command codes, now White's in the wind," Hugo said. "He was already putting another crew together, or he had another ship running all along."

Sun looked down at the display on her small forearm band and shook her head. "You really are trying to take the Angel for yourself. Did this all really come from White?"

"Yes, the records to back it up are in the message with your share of what he was skimming from our jobs," Spin said. "Everyone got their fair share according to the crew hierarchy, except for me, I just took the bounty he made by turning me in."

"What about Sun? Nigel?" Hugo asked.

"You don't really know me, Lieutenant," Spin spat the last at Hugo. "But I take care of my people, and that's what I'll use most of that money for."

Sun strode towards Spin. "For all this to work, we have to do it by the rules the entire crew agreed to follow. The vote, splitting the money, dealing with the Captain, it's twisted now. The crew has been given all this ready cash, enough for them to all buy their own small ships, and Dorian has made sure that White won't poke his head out for a very long time. You've forgotten your place, little girl, and it has cost us all dearly."

Spin made a conscious choice and an incredible effort to see past her anger. There were people counting on her, and out of all of them, Sun was the one who could best take care of herself. "White was corrupt, he turned us in, so he was already about to get spooked. I sent records and the money the crew deserves to them to back that up," Spin said with an increasing level of calm. "I did not send Dorian."

Leland, Jorin and Nigel carried what was left of Dorian into the Fleet Feather, and Spin paused to watch before continuing. "Now you're telling me you would have held some or all of the Angel crew's money back so they would return to the ship and vote you up as Captain."

"Me or Hugo, either one of us would lead the Angel honestly," she said.

"Politics. Pure politics of the worst kind." Spin looked past Sun to Hugo. "I want you to gather the corpses of the crew members who were sent here to tear my ship up along with what's left of the rest, and the First Officer, and go. Being a part of that crew, being near leaders from that crew has cost me and the people I love enough."

"Bodies?" Hugo asked as he rushed to the shed, two crewmen behind him.

"Under the tarp. I'm keeping one of their exo frames," Spin said coldly. Her hand found the gun strapped to her thigh, and she rested her hand on it. Her gaze locked with Sun's. "Someone sent a bunch of the loading staff from the Angel to get their First Officer, you weren't available, so Nigel and I took care of it. I would have talked them down, or even bribed them, but the knuckleheads weren't very talkative while they were tearing the Feather apart. Where were you?"

"I was in a meeting with the Angel Lieutenants," Sun said. "Discussing what White did to us."

"It doesn't matter now," Spin said. "Neither do you. The trust is broken. When that shuttle takes off, I want you on it."

Spin turned towards the Fleet Feather and started walking.

"Aspen, you have to see how badly you screwed all of this up, and how I can be led to think that you're running a one-woman coup for the Angel."

"I was, but it was so you would get the votes, even if the crew were on their way off ship to spend the pile of money I sent them," she replied. "But now that we're taking inventory of mistakes, how about considering someone who would slip her friend medication without checking to see if it had a genetic component?" Spin stopped and half turned. "That dose triggered a genetic anti-tampering measure. You cost me, maybe as much as nine months. Now I don't have time to forgive people like you, and I have to work on another plan."

"What? I didn't know, I'm so-"

"Not knowing is no excuse for not taking the time to find out when it's my life you're playing with. I don't have time for you, Sun. Go help your fellow Lieutenant with the dead."

"You can't seriously think you can lead anyone, just look at what happened today, and you don't have a plan."

"Today is your failure," Spin said. "And as for a plan, I'm

going to get a fast ship before the Authority finds out we're here, then blast for British controlled space. I'll leave whoever isn't up for the next part there, where slavery is illegal and they'll be free. Then I'm going to Geist. If there's a cure, it'll be there." The whole plan was fabricated on the spot, but Spin had to admit to herself that every word of it felt right. "You can stay here, or sign up with the Angel crew. I don't care."

"Come with me, we'll get this sorted out. The goodwill you've earned with whoever stays aboard will go a long way, you won't even serve under me anymore."

"You want me to believe that a profiteer crew would go to Geist, one of the most dangerous places in the galaxy, without the promise of a rich target? We both know better." Far behind Sun, four crewmembers from the Angel worked to load the bodies in the back, while Hugo untied the survivors inside the shed. "You'd better go help your crew. I'd hate to think of the impression you'd make during this tragic time. Losing the Captain and crewmembers on the same day. They'll need strong leadership."

"Aspen," Sun said, pleadingly.

"Goodbye," Spin replied, walking through the hatch and closing it behind. She rushed to the infirmary, where she was shocked by the sight of Leland working elbow deep in Dorian's chest. "How is he?"

"His brain was saved, in emergency stasis. I'm just working on getting the container free of his body. It'll be good for another twenty hours. The damage he took is incredible, whoever did this must think he's dead."

"What do you need to keep his grey matter working, doc?" Nigel asked.

"I'm not a doctor," Leland said, smiling a little. "A long term stasis medium with the systems to go with it would do the job nicely. A new body for this guy would be better, but that would take time, a specialist and a lot of money. I have to be honest, there are some interfaces I could hook him up to, but I've done everything my conscience demands of me. He'll be stable, in storage once we get the support vessel, but I don't care about restoring him."

"This is one of my oldest friends," Nigel said. "I'll pay you to get him installed in something that gets him up and moving again, don't worry."

"That's if we can trust him," Leland replied. "You can't trust a man with more than one master, and I think Dorian had at least two."

"We'll face that situation if it ever comes up. There's no time to go body shopping right now," Spin said, "but I'm sure you can find the stasis system you need in the market here."

"I can go do that, I'll be finished here in a couple minutes. I'll need a few credits though," Leland said.

"What about him?" Spin asked, nodding towards Keith, who laid in the other bed with his legs inside corrective casts.

"Him? He's been pretending to sleep since we dragged Dorian in here," Leland replied. "He's done, ready to walk out. His bones are still knitting, but the reconstruction casts can keep working while he hobbles around on crutches."

"I was half asleep," Keith replied. "You want me to leave with these things still working?"

"There's a shuttle outside with Hugo and Sun, they need a First Officer to interrogate about Captain White's hidden money and the betrayal of crewmembers," Spin said.

Keith's eyes widened and he recoiled slightly as Spin described the crimes. It started as soon as she mentioned hidden money. "I was about to retire as First Officer, move on to better things. I could pay you quite a bit if you sent me in the other direction. I have a small ship ready."

"If you could barter time, that would be a done deal, but money happens to be the one thing I don't need right now." She crossed the room and started to help him out of bed, only to be frantically pushed away.

"No! Do you know what they'll do to me?"

"Can I have a few volunteers to take this trash out the airlock?" Spin called over her shoulder.

"Okay, I got it, hold that box open," Leland said as he withdrew a black box from the Dorian's chest cavity.

Nigel held a metal box open and watched the container with his old friend's brain slip inside. "Can he feel anything?" he asked.

"His mind is in complete hibernation. When we plug him back in to something compatible, he'll just be missing some time," Leland closed the lid and sighed. "Okay, we're safe to drag this guy off the ship," he said, looking at Keith.

Mirra cracked her knuckles in the doorway. "Said you needed help with this?"

Spin could only step aside as Nigel, Leland, Jorin and Mirra carried Keith as he protested and spat curses. They walked him down the ship's debarkation ramp and nearly dropped him on the pavement. "Here's your First Officer," Spin said to Hugo, who rushed over to the Fleet Feather. "I'm pretty sure he was in on everything White did, so you'll have someone to hang after the funeral tonight."

"The Cool Angel is an important ship," He said as he helped Keith to his feet. "It doesn't matter who takes the role of Captain, you'll want friends aboard and this is not the way to make them."

"I don't have time to care," Spin said. "Besides, I'm starting to see how dirty your ship is. You knew all about the Captain skimming, didn't you?"

Hugo struggled with Keith, who was a head shorter and much thinner.

Spin didn't wait for an answer. "Expect to get found out. Good luck." She closed the ramp way.

"So, what now, Captain?" Nigel asked.

When she turned around, she found that everyone on the Fleet Feather had come to the main passenger cabin. They were all looking at her expectantly. "There is no time for any elegant solutions. This ship won't take us into space again because I'm going to buy another. While I do that, Leland and Nigel will go get the parts we need to keep Dorian alive and restore our Long Runner, just in case."

"What about hiding here? It's a good world, there are safe places here and there," Jorin asked. "I mean, I want to go with you, but some of you have money and can afford to hide out."

"We all have a slave mark, and five more United Core Authority ships just entered orbit," Mitchell said. "None of us are safe here."

"We have to be off world in two hours," Spin said. "We need to pack provisions into anything we can use as a crate. That's food, water, survival gear, tools, and then you can move on to other things you want to keep from this ship. Start packing the essentials into the Long Runner."

"Where is this new ship going, Spin?" Leland asked as he wiped his hands on a sterilizing cloth.

"British Alliance Territory," Spin answered. "The safest place for us. Whoever wants to leave then will get paid and can start a new life. I only have three months left before my clock runs out now, so I'm going to Geist to see if there's a cure for people like me. If anyone wants to follow me then you're more than welcome."

"I've watched a doll die before. I don't want to see that again," Leland said. "I'm in."

"Heroism looks good on me," Nigel said. "How about it, Governor?" he asked Mitchell.

"He's going home to see what he can salvage," Spin answered for him. "I bet he'll be back in his place before long, and we'll need someone in the British Government."

"That's the best way for me to help," he agreed. "There's a younger version of me who so much wants to go with you, but you're right. It's more important that I tell my entire government what the Countess did, and prove that I'm still alive."

Spin saw Mirra and Della whispering to each other, they looked like they were coming to a conclusion. "I don't need everyone to decide now," she told them. "Let's just focus on getting out of here before the Authority catches up to us."

TWENTY-TWO

The dealership was happy to send a shuttle to pick her up when Spin told them that she was looking to make 'a more substantial purchase' and the pilot seemed relieved when she told her that she had work to do on the way. There was one more thing she had to do for the crew of the Cool Angel, and she managed to finish as the shuttle touched down inside the docking bay of the outer orbit station the dealership owned. There was a field of vessels of all different makes and shapes, but she refused to let herself become distracted as she finished putting her story together on her computer.

The story she told was simple. Months before she was captured, Captain White had her set up money laundering accounts with alien banks within days of him finding out that she knew how to do that kind of work. She left herself a back-door, burying her name in the documents as his spouse. Her crewmates and her were betrayed by Captain White to the United Core Authority and he was paid a bounty. She included the transaction evidence. It was also clear that he had been skimming credits from the crew's share of whatever gains the ship made for at least a few years. She included that evidence as well, even though most of the crew already had it. She gave the crew all his hidden money. Spin also added that she didn't send Dorian, but that she'd just met him and he probably had his own mission.

At the end of her story she apologized for not being able to rescue everyone who was captured along with her, and humbly stated that she was leaving the Cool Angel crew to pursue another course. That was, the pursuit of a cure for herself since she didn't have long to live, for other people like her, and to help everyone with a slave's mark find freedom until her final day.

As the shuttle docked to the heavily armed, but modestly sized station, she sent the message. Spin was surprised at the pang of loss, or regret that accompanied the act, but she was happy that her side would arrive on the communicators of all of her old crewmates, even if they were too far away to get it for several days.

"We've arrived, Ma'am," the pilot said. The airlock opened, and a gentleman in a spotless business suit with a long jacket smiled at her from the other side. "Spin?"

"That's me," she said as she made her way through the airlock.

"It's good to meet you, I'm Ligig, one of the managers here. I'm surprised to see you came alone."

"The rest of my crew is busy," she replied. "It's moving day."

"That must be exciting," Ligig said. She noticed that his

eyes and lips were a little too large for a human. "So we need to set you up with a ship today then, and it has to be able to do?"

"Everything," Spin said as she noticed that he only had two thick fingers but a perfect human thumb. "It has to have armour, military class shields, weapons, faster than light capability and room for twenty with cargo space. It has to be ready today."

The light hearted mannerisms of the manager faded a little. "We do have what you're looking for, but you realize that documenting the sale could be difficult. We checked on you before you arrived."

"I have a slave's mark," Spin said. "Can you issue ownership documentation using the British system?"

"Well, yes, just like we did with the shuttle we sold you earlier, but for a ship like this, the transmission and certification will take weeks. You could fly the ship off the lot, but it won't technically be yours, even according to the British Alliance because it will take time for it to be put on record."

"That doesn't change much for me or my crew," Spin said, turning to face Ligig. "We all have slave's marks, and we'll be using this to get to British territory, to start a new life. I just need the power to protect them while we get out of here."

She was surprised to see such a clear expression of sympathy from the manager. "I understand bondage," he said. "It may not be obvious, but I am Issyrian from the Ponolu Clutch. My people remember being captured for research a long time ago. I'll help you. Come with me."

Spin was shown down a hallway that ended in a circular platform surrounded by transparent metal. The light of the distant sun bounced off the hulls of over a hundred ships floating in neat rows. She could see tiny holographic projectors along the edge of the platform. "So, you really have what I need?"

"Yes, how much do you have to spend?" he asked.

She smiled at him. "How much for your best?"

"That is the Tee Five Seven One, four hundred eighty million platinum," he replied. "It's the last attack ship built by Rage Shipyards."

"Okay, that's a lot more than I can spend."

"It is beyond what you requested anyway," Ligig said. "So, a great ship, but no loss to you. I would recommend lot number three zero zero one, The Convoy King Mark Three." He summoned a projection of a hybrid tug and cargo hauler. "The powerful shields can expand to cover exterior blocks of containers extending from the sides of the ship. It has a field emitter that can create a cushion or hauling beam that will prevent a collision or allow you to pull many times the Convoy King's mass. With the current configuration, you can fit a crew of fifty if you include the passenger area. The fixtures are old, and we have yet to equip the passenger area with any mattresses or linens – the old ones had to be destroyed – but it's bigger than you need. For cargo you can use the included armoured space or attach hundreds of extra-large containers. Weapons are a bit of a problem. It only has three paired heavy cannons on separately shielded rotary turrets. There were more, but those ports had to be capped since we did not have the time to build replacement guns. On the brighter side, there are twenty-eight recessed large missile launcher ports that come loaded with seeker rounds. They're a fairly basic weapon, but you could load whatever fits. Most likely not exactly what you're looking for there, but it would be a match for anything in its class. Find a good arms dealer who has some standard turrets available, and you could increase the ship's firepower many times over."

"Does it have any docking space?" Spin asked, already becoming comfortable with the fact that she would not be able to afford the ship.

"Yes, plenty for its size. The Convoy King series has been used as a remote mothership and main rescue vessel because it comes with eight or more small launch bays depending on its configuration. There is no servicing area for landing ships though, so you have to seal bays off if you need to repair shuttles or fighters."

Spin looked at the hologram of the blocky, dark hulled utilitarian ship, trying not to like it and failing. "Condition?"

"Fully reconditioned except for the passenger area. That was next on our list. It was cleaned, the damage was repaired, and we were about to add higher end fixtures and other creature comforts. The power plant, hull, and all the essentials including the captain's and crew quarters are as they should be. In perfect condition."

"This was salvaged from an area under artificial intelligence control?"

"Pulled out of the war zone after the UCA finished neutralizing the area. The bots aboard killed the crew when they were infected by the virus, then left the ship to find other victims. The captain of this vessel was fast enough to lock the reactors down as the machines turned on them. An old fashioned safety measure, but it saved the vessel. Too bad it couldn't save the crew. We have done the work on this, and checked the history. No one is looking for this ship, and the UCA was paid the salvage fee for it. The ticket is on record and available."

Spin closed her eyes and braced herself. "How much?"

"Two hundred and ten million," he replied. "But worth every platinum coin."

It was only a little more than she had, but enough so even if she bargained, she'd be down to nothing. "Let's keep looking," she said. For twenty long minutes, she was shown ship after ship, most of them were not nearly as well armed, and the few that were would take even more work. What was worse, any good solution still drained her funds to desperate levels.

"This is not going well for you," Ligig said sadly. "Or I'm showing you the wrong ships."

"Can I see the Convoy King again?" Spin said.

He brought the hologram of the bulky ship up in front of them. "It is a nice ship, every pirate and long hauling company has been looking at it."

"But no one buys it," Spin said. "Why?"

"The excellent condition demands a certain price," Ligig replied.

"I'll give you one hundred and forty million, I can transmit the funds in less than a minute," she told him. "That's real platinum for something your company probably salvaged for thirty."

"It's too low," Ligig said. "I would get in trouble for this, but one hundred ninety."

Spin was relieved to hear a price she could afford. She'd be down to less than ten percent of her funds, but it was within her range. "This isn't going to just be a ship, it'll be important, do important work. I'm planning on calling it the Ponolu Princess, because it's a good name for a ship that frees slaves, running them straight to the British Alliance. One hundred fifty."

"You must be a fool if you think I'll believe that, but you're an amusing fool, so I will accept one hundred eighty-five."

Spin smiled at him and watched his expression for a long moment. There was a price he'd take, she just had to observe him, figure out how close she was and offer a little less. She wished she had more time to barter, she was starting to really like him. "You like shapeshifting into humans," she said. "I'll give you a scan of myself so you can practice looking like me if you like, and I have a ship to trade. It's in bad shape, and stolen, but I'm sure someone with your connections can do something with it." She projected an image of the Fleet Feather as it was when she left it half an hour before. "Luxury ship, very expensive. It won't have any linens or mattresses inside though."

"I can't give you much, we'll only tear it apart," he said. "And as for the image of you, well, you are interesting."

Spin decided it was time to take a guess at what he would accept, a real offer. "A hundred forty-nine million, a scan of me, my old ship, and your crew helps us move so we can be on our way. You get paid right now."

Ligig looked at her with a twitch, then back to the image of the Feather, then back to her. "Yes, I can do that."

"You can do it now?" Spin asked.

He brought up an ownership transfer interface with the British Alliance certification numbers already entered in. "You transfer the platinum, or the credits, and I will transfer the ship, get my people working."

Spin sent him the entire payment. "Done."

TWENTY-THREE

For the first time in her life, Spin felt nervous about spending money. The realization that she'd just spent a sizable fortune without setting foot on the deck of a ship she needed to carry her friends to safety set in when she boarded the shuttle to return to the planet below. It seemed like Ligig was being true to his word though.

Before she left he politely summoned what seemed like everyone in the station, at least thirty people were gathering in the embarkation area of the station, where several airlocks were lined up for arriving shuttles, taking orders and calling more support in. Everything was in motion, she only hoped that she didn't get robbed in her hastiness.

"I've got a problem," came Nigel's garbled voice over her communicator. The high priority of the message allowed him to speak directly to her without waiting for her to answer.

"I'm here," Spin replied, watching the shuttle transition from fiery entry to blue skies. "What's going on?"

"We're behind the people-parts store-"

"I told you not to call it that," she heard Leland say in the background.

"The cybernetics place, we got everything we need, but there are Authority soldiers blocking every direction. Crap, one's stepping into the store right now. What do I do? I could shoot my way out, but the brain case Leland's carrying is pretty delicate, and it's bulky. Oh, and it was expensive."

"Find another store nearby and hide there, find their back door."

"Won't we get trapped if they're watching the walkways?" Nigel asked.

"Whatever will keep you out of their direct line of sight. I'm on my way," Spin finished. "Pilot, do you think you could land here?" she said, pointing at a map with Nigel's location projected from her arm.

"I can land just up the street, but it won't be a place I can stay on the ground. If there's trouble, I'll have to hover above, unless they start paying too much attention to me, then I'll have to get out of there."

"That's fine," Spin said. "I'll give you a hundred platinum if you drop me off, then pick me and my friends up while we run away from the United Core Authority."

"A hundred fifty, and you got it. My name is Sharon, by the way. Hang on."

It felt as though her stomach leapt up into her throat as the shuttle tipped down and dropped at an enormous speed. She didn't slow their decent until they were under one thousand meters, and the landing was so soft, Spin barely felt it. "Thanks, I'll be back," Spin said as she got out of the shuttle. A clothing vendor with racks of outerwear along the front of their shop gave her an idea, and she snagged a long hooded cloak as she passed, stopping in front of the owner. "How much?"

"Twenty-five plat," he replied.

She pressed the coins into his hand and wrapped the cloak around herself, raising the hood. At a glance she counted three Authority soldiers on the street, all of them were watching people go by, and she assumed that included facial scanning, at least. Sidestepping the first two was easy, a crowd of adolescents ran behind them, forcing them to step away from the side of the street, and she ran along with them, squeezing behind the soldiers.

The third was an entirely different story. He was standing in an alleyway that led directly to the tight walkway Nigel and Leland were trapped on. Their options were becoming more limited by the minute, as Authority soldiers split up, visiting different stores. She was running out of time. If Nigel wasn't just being paranoid, then he and Leland would be caught.

"Get ready to pick me up," Spin said over her comm to Sharon. "Nigel, Leland, I have a shuttle supporting us. If there's a commotion, break for the big four-way double lane to the north, you see it?"

"I do, but be careful, this place is crawling."

"There's no way to carefully kick the hornet's nest," Spin replied. She dropped her hood and straightened up as she walked towards the guard in her way. The markings on his uniform designated him as a Sergeant. "Excuse me," she said in her sweetest voice. "My masters sent me here to check prices on the jewellery here, and I think I'm in the wrong place." She lightly rested her hand on his chest and regarded him with her best lost look. If his people were looking for her and her crew, then she'd know it right away. "Is there a jeweller here?"

He grinned at her and, taking her hand, he turned her to face the east side of the market. "You're about ten minutes' walk away from where you have to be. There's an old emergency shelter that someone turned into a jeweller, and I hear it's the best one here."

"Old shelter?" Spin asked, looking uncertain. With timid steps, she guided the soldier away from the alley, his back was already facing it. Nigel and Leland took advantage of the opening, quietly rushing through.

"Oh, don't worry, they gussied the place up, you can't even tell what it was, but it's safe, not like this place."

"I feel very safe with all your soldiers around," she replied, giving his hand a little squeeze.

"Oh, there are only a couple of us actually on duty, most are just here to shop. We're at the end of our rotation on the ground for the day."

Nigel and Leland were being paranoid, she realized. Most of the soldiers didn't care who anyone was, they were too busy shopping. "Thank you so much," she said, starting to withdraw her hand.

He gripped her fingers, looking her up and down. The draw of her needy expression and candied voice could only distract him from what she wore, and how well armed she was for so long, and he obviously caught a glance at something in her cloak. Most likely the weapon strapped to her thigh.

"Who's your master?"

"Why do you ask?"

"I've come into an inheritance, and I'd like to make an offer on you."

"You couldn't afford me," Spin replied, doing her best to laugh lightly at the offer.

"It was a big inheritance," he said. "I'll scan you and find out myself."

She yanked her fingers from his grip, seized his wrist, turned and flipped him over her shoulder. "Run!" she shouted at Nigel and Leland, who were ten steps down the main street. She kicked him in the face as hard as she could, then used the opportunity to steal his gun, his restraints and a pouch from the inside of his jacket. "Emergency!" he shouted, probably into a communicator she couldn't see, not so much to the guards on the street. He grabbed her leg and she kicked her other one as high as she could, missing his head by a centimetre, then she brought it down with all the weight and force she could, landing the back edge of her heel in his right eye socket.

Free from his grip, she tossed his weapon, kept the restraints and drew her weapon. "Down with the Masters!" she shouted, blasting the air and breaking into a run. The chaos was enough cover to get her to the crossroads, where the shuttle was setting down, the side hatch opening. "Our ride!" she shouted at Nigel and Leland from behind. "That's our ride!"

Bolts of white energy sizzled past her, and she peered over her shoulder to see three United Core Authority soldiers taking aim at her and the shuttle. Spin turned towards them, and fired at the one that didn't have several innocent civilians in the way. She had time to take several shots, missing but driving him back under cover behind a ramshackle public bathroom. With a turn and a roll, she was back on her feet, lurching towards the shuttle and finally diving at the hatch.

Sharon blasted off from the ground before the hatch was closed, leaving the chaos behind. "They were just shopping, guys. The whole unit was just buying things for their girlfriends and picking up souvenirs," she told Nigel.

"How could we know?" Nigel said with a shrug.

"Why was that one after you?" Leland asked.

"He wanted to buy me from my masters, and when I wouldn't tell him who my owners were, he started scanning me. Couldn't take the risk that we're wanted, and even if we're not wanted yet, that he'd see I'm far from home and mark me as an escaped slave. That's probably happening right now anyway."

Spin settled into her seat and looked through the forward viewport. Their pilot was guiding them on a smooth, low course through a high mountain range barely above the trees. "We're going to our original destination, the Fleet Feather. Sorry about the detour and trouble."

"No worries, I haven't had that much fun in weeks," Sharon replied over her shoulder.

"Nigel, can you fly the type of ship Spin just bought? What was it, the Convoy King?"

"Barely, that's huge, I've never been allowed near the controls of something like that," he replied.

"Spin?"

"I know how, I've just never done it for real," Spin replied.

Leland nodded at the pilot seat in front of him. "I wonder?"

"Hey, Sharon," Spin said, moving to the co-pilot's seat. "Have you ever flown-"

"A rig like you just got the slip for?" she finished. "All the time. You don't have a pilot, do you?"

"I can pay you," Spin said.

"You'd have to buy me," she replied. "That's why I had so much fun back there, I loved watching you kick that officer and get away."

"Would you like to fly us to British Alliance territory and get freed by the government there?"

"Don't play with me here, even if you can afford me, the sale wouldn't be official, you're escaped slaves too, from the sound of it," Sharon replied.

"Let me worry about that, I'm just wondering if you'd like to come with us."

"To British territory? Yes."

"Then give me your master's ident. I'll contact him."

"Sure, but I'm not getting my hopes up. His name is Derek Menor. He's the only one in the system."

Spin looked him up and found that he was part owner of the dealership she bought her ships from, then checked the slave market to see what registered pilots were worth. She was surprised to find that the average was only twenty-five thousand platinum, and that there were thousands on the market. "This is an interested buyer, I'm interested in purchasing your slave, Sharon's freedom. This will be a black market exchange. Contact me immediately, you know who I am and what my money is worth to your company already," Spin said into her communicator.

"That'll get his attention," Sharon said. "He's one of the greediest people I've ever met. So, the deal is you pay for my freedom and I fly you over the British territorial line."

"Yes, we need a pilot and I have a feeling about you."

"I'll do it then, but Derek will probably just ignore-"

Spin's arm display lit up with a reply in text: MAKE AN OFFER. She replied: TWICE THE AVERAGE, FIFTY THOUSAND.

The reply came back only seconds later through voice communication. "She's worth five times that much, I've put a lot of time and training into her, made her a great pilot and a better late night companion, if you know what I mean. That took a lot of time, and a lot of patience."

"I'm only interested in making her free," Spin said.

"Oh, you're a woman and you're not looking to own her? Then she's wasted on you, don't call again, bitch." The call ended.

"I'm sorry," Spin said quietly. "Any chance you'd run?"

"Work and patience, my ass," Sharon said, furious. Regardless of her state, she still set the shuttle down beside the Fleet Feather smoothly. Half a dozen bots moved from the back of the Feather carrying bins to a bulk transport shuttle as Mirra, Della, Mitchel, and Joren loaded them with everything they could. "I learned everything – and I mean everything – myself or with experienced friends. The only reason why I don't run is because he has a tracker on me."

"I could deactivate that for you," Leland said. "Most likely."

"I don't even care anymore. I'll go with you if you'll take on another escaped slave, it seems like that's what you do, anyway."

"You're more than welcome, we're beating a hasty retreat anyway," Spin replied.

"Okay, there will be a tracker on your new ship, by the way. I'll help you disable them as soon as we get into our first wormhole. You have a pilot," Sharon said, shaking Spin's hand. "I'm not even going back for the few things he lets me keep under my bed."

"You know, that's the only reason why I feel bad about leaving the Cool Angel, leaving my toolbox behind," Nigel said. "Anyway, welcome to the crew, see you up there."

"Thanks, guys. I'm still pissed that Derek took credit for, well, me, so I might seem a little ungrateful, but it'll wear off."

"So, how does this go?" Spin asked.

"I wait here, pretend you're keeping me with you until it's time to go to your new ship, then when you're ready to go, I fly you up there, send my shuttle back on autopilot – the long way – and take off with you. Your ship is being prepped right now, so other than moving your stuff from your old ship here, it's already good to go."

"One minute," Spin said. "Mirra, do we have all the essentials on that cargo shuttle?"

"We did what you said, all our favourite stuff, the bedding, mattresses, anything we can sell at another port, supplies and cash stores. All we have left are the clothes and the non-essential luxuries, like rare soaps. The last of the medical supplies just got loaded, we were about to move on to the last stuff."

"God, that's fast," Leland said.

"Okay, tell them they can close the doors and go. We're going up to the ship, get aboard my shuttle."

"But there's thousands of credits' worth in luxury stuff here," Mira replied. "Are you sure? Maybe fifty thousand or so."

"Leave it, we have to go," Spin replied.

"Don't forget Dorian!" Leland added from the back seat.

TWENTY-FOUR

The Long Runner, the moving shuttle and the Dealership's shuttle each fit in the Convoy King's launch bays. There were four on either side of the segment of the ship right behind the forward section. The hologram that Spin saw did not reflect how big the ship actually was. She was about to say that she wished she got something more compact to her crew, but then she noticed that every one of them were looking through the broad window of the shuttle, gawking at their new ship. So she asked; "What do you think?" instead.

"I'm still processing," Nigel said as the door to the launch bay they landed in closed, clamps secured their shuttle, and the air pressure outside increased.

"It's a little, um, square?" Della said.

"I think she means industrial," Mirra added.

"Right, industrial. It looks like something you'd haul metal in."

"You could," Jorin added. "I mean, I used to help my dad find haulers for big mining corporations all the time, there was a lot of money in that."

"But dirty, right?" Della said.

"Well, for a couple guys, but most of the crew never touched the ore. For them it was all about living aboard and making the run without any trouble then getting paid."

"Oh," Della replied.

The whole group made their way off the shuttle and started through the dim hallways. They were utilitarian, but most of the pipes and cables were only visible through intermittent transparent panels on the walls. Spin could tell the thin metal panelling could be removed easily, and remembered that the main hallway ran the whole length of the ship, offering easy access to all the core systems. "There are two decks in most of the segments, three in the fore segment with the bridge, the primary emitter and communication systems. Oh, and the crew quarters are in the forward segment too. About half of our cargo space was converted for long term passengers, but that's back there, in the segment behind us. I was told there are no beds or other creature comforts there, so we have a place to put all the stuff we took from the Fleet Feather."

"If that space is nicer than the crew quarters, can I move in?" Della asked, earning a sharp elbowing from Mirra.

"You said you wouldn't complain," Mirra whispered harshly.

"I'm just asking."

"You can," Spin said, nodding with a smile. "Since you won't be critical to the bridge, that's not a problem. You'll have to visit us in segment one though."

"I'll keep it nice and clean and cook at least two hot meals," Della replied.

"All right, can you, Mirra and Leland make sure the unpacking happens fast. Just have them offload our stuff to the landing bay across from the one they're in, we'll have to settle for that. Take this," Spin said, handing her old sidearm to Mirra. "It should stun any of the bots for at least a few seconds. If we have to get out of here before they're finished and they freak out because we're leaving before they can return to base."

"So, I shoot the bots if they start freaking out or running for an airlock, then hit their power switches," Mirra said.

"What do we do if the bots freak out?" Della asked.

"We hide," Leland said. "Unless you have another of those blasters."

"There should be a couple somewhere in our stuff, but I don't know where," Spin replied.

"I'll watch for it," Leland replied as the trio started down the hallway towards the landing bay behind them.

"Okay, time for most of us to get to the bridge," Spin said. "Nigel, head aft to the main power plant and tell me how things look back there."

"On my way," Nigel said excitedly before she finished telling him.

THE BRIDGE WAS EXTREMELY WELL ORGANIZED in the centre. It wasn't like the Cool Angel's, where the captain sat in the middle on a raised seat that was more like a throne. The captain's seat was more well-padded than the others aboard her new ship, but it was set in the middle of a large control console that had two comfortable looking but less grand seats to either side.

"Pilot's station," Sharon said. "Just like I remember when I moved this ship in. The security umbilical has already been released, and we are in standby, holding station." She slipped into the seat to the right of the captain's chair, gesturing towards it. "Take your place, Captain."

Spin hesitated a moment, looking at all the status panels in front of the padded chair. She looked behind her at the four stations that looked different, newer and less complicated. They were set against either side of the rear half of the modest bridge in pairs. "What are those?"

"That's the weapon's package. Only two of those stations are running, the other ones are waiting for more cannons to be installed." Sharon replied. "This ship used to be a lot more dangerous, it could be again if you find a good weapons' dealer."

"So no one can fire weapons from the main stations?" Spin asked as she slipped into the comfortable captain's seat. It adjusted to her size, pushing the back forward. The cushions didn't adjust, they didn't have to, they were wonderfully plush.

"We can fire two turrets and the missile banks, but the controls up here are wave panels, they track your hands as you follow targets, so they take concentration. It's not what you want people at these stations doing, since we control things like shields, power distribution, flying the ship, you know, that stuff."

Jorin dropped into the seat to Spin's left and activated the main screen. "Status of bays, crew reports, maintenance records, life support status, panel sensors for our armour, shield controls, communications and our Navnet profile."

"You know how to work with that?" Spin asked, surprised. Jorin had been helpful in support of any basic work since he decided to stay, but she hadn't seen him take charge of anything.

"Everything but the shield controls. I have no idea what any of that stuff means. Besides, I think it's more to raise and lower sections of the shields so people can come and go from our little landing bays, rather than managing defence."

Spin looked at the control panel and nodded. "You're right. You couldn't screw us up with anything there, shield wise. I'm surprised it looks so well set up."

"I'm not," Sharon said. "This ship is made so a few crewmembers can take care of the whole ship, just like any hauler. The difference is that it's also a tug, so we've got hard lines we can launch at other ships and energy fields that take someone who knows what they're doing."

"Hey, I've got someone coming in a four-man planet hopper," Jorin said. "Transmission incoming."

"Hey, Spin," said an image of Sun as it appeared at the front of the bridge. "Listen, I'm sorry about everything. The truth is already coming out, and I jumped to conclusions. I was getting ready to fend off competition for the Captain's chair on the Angel, and I turned on you without thinking."

Spin took a breath, looked at the captain's station in front of her. It was populated with status displays summarizing the condition and all activity on the ship, as well as readouts and controls for all the core systems. Aside from that, there were plenty of icons and features she didn't know anything about. She was still angry with Sun, but her head had cleared enough for her to know that she'd regret leaving things the way she did.

"We had a communication breakdown in a few ways, it's cost us enough already."

"Should I clear her to dock?" Jorin asked, looking pleased at having a job already.

"Yes," Spin said.

"Bay seven," Jorin told her.

"I'll meet you," Spin said, leaving the Captain's seat. Sun's image disappeared, leaving the large transparent metal window that wrapped around three quarters of the bridge.

"Captain? Who's in charge while you're off the bridge?" Sharon asked.

"Him," she said passing the Governor as he walked through the door. "Think you can make a few decisions if something comes up?"

"I served in the British Alliance for five years, so I might manage," he replied.

Spin arched an eyebrow. "Really?"

"Don't get excited, I was in logistics, mostly serving from an office," he said. "How do you think I found politics?"

"Spin, Spin!" she heard through her communicator, it was Nigel.

"Yes?"

"This ship is awesome! I'm standing beside a purring X Four Twenty reactor and its seven brothers. The service tags say these things were checked and worked on last week. We're good to go, and man, are we ever going to go!"

"Good, do you have to stay back there while we're under way, or are you better being on the bridge?"

"I'm going to set myself up here. There are bunks for engineering staff too, so I'll stay close to these babies," he replied. "You picked a good one."

Spin watched as Sun emerged from her tiny shuttle. It looked like it was dug out of a mud pit, and Spin couldn't count the dents on the thin hull panels. "I bought the cheapest shuttle I could find," Sun explained as she came through the door carrying five bags. Spin took two. "I was able to get Nigel, Boro and Trevor's most important stuff from the Angel before I left. They let me do that much."

"What happened?" Spin asked.

"They already had the vote, Keith didn't want to wait, and since he was still effectively First Officer, he got his way. The crew heard me, Hugo and him out, then Lieutenant Newson said her piece remotely since she was still on her way. The crew voted her up to the Captain's chair, so she's taking the Angel. It's not as good as Hugo, not as bad as Keith moving up, but it's not good either. Her first act was to order Keith's execution, and then hold a vote about keeping escaped slaves off the crew."

"Seriously?" Spin asked, surprised.

"She argued that escaped slaves would always bring trouble to our door, and the Cool Angel couldn't pretend to be a legitimate trade ship while one or more of us were aboard. The vote passed, I can't even start over as an able crewmember."

Spin resisted the urge to tell her; 'so that's why you're here.' Instead she told her; "You're welcome here. I'm going to need you to teach me a few things as my First Officer though. I can't serve as captain if I don't know what half my command display is trying to tell me."

"You have a deal," Sun said.

"Problem, I have a blinking ship heading towards us, it's yellow, and uh..." Jorin announced over the ship intercom.

"Something's coming at us with weapons and shields charged," Sun said. She dropped the bags and followed Spin as she ran for the bridge.

Mitchell turned the captain's seat towards her, and Spin dropped into it. "Where do you want me?" he asked.

"Man the guns, Governor," she replied.

"I can do that," he replied.

Sun pushed Jorin out of his seat and pointed to the one on the end of the console. "Press the Status Screen button on that station and you'll be able to do everything you were doing before." She made a quick series of adjustments to her station and it became a First Officer's interface with combat shield controls, missile system access, a damage control interface and navigation information.

"Sharon, time to go," Spin said. With a dull roar sounding throughout the ship, their vessel came to life, turning away from the dealership station and thrusting away. "I'll start the worm-hole calculations."

"Shields up, setting up a power reserve for the Governor so he doesn't run out of juice while he's shooting," Sun said. "It's a United Core Authority Light Cruiser."

"I have a transmission from that ship incoming," Jorin said.

"Put it on," Spin said.

"Hello, I can't believe it's actually you, Aspen," said a squat man in the uniform of a United Core Authority Captain. "Our records showed that you were returned to your owner, but somehow one of our people scanned you down there. I've never heard of a doll escaping twice."

"I'm special," Spin said. "What can I do for you?"

"You can power down and allow us to board. I promise you the best treatment we can provide in our brig. You are charged with grand theft, assaulting an officer, and grand theft. That is if that's Sharon Fiora beside you. I have a warrant for your arrest, and for the arrest of anyone with you as co-conspirators."

"I have other plans, so I'll get back to you," Spin said, finding the control that would end the call on her station and pushing it. "Can we take that ship?"

"Right now? With no training and barely any familiarity with this ship?" Sun asked. "No."

A flurry of particle beam bursts passed near their hull, lighting up the window as they faded into the darkness. "Warning shots," Spin said. "Can we at least damage their shields?" she asked, looking at the weapons status on her station and highlighting the missile system. They had eighteen heavy electromagnetic pulse rockets loaded in their rapid fire launchers.

"This ship has a heavy launch system?" Sun asked, surprised. "Yes, yes! Those are cheap, give 'em hell."

Spin selected their port launcher and opened it. "I'm here, I'm here," Mirra said as she ran into the bridge and sat at the weapons station beside the Governor. "What do you need?"

"Countermeasures, make sure the anti-missile battery is programmed, and if it isn't, get ready to target manually," Sun said.

"Spin?" Mirra asked.

"Go ahead, she's our First Officer," Spin confirmed. She watched as the missile bay doors finished swinging open and launched all nine heavy missiles. They rocketed into view for a few seconds before turning, spreading out and seeking the UCA Light Cruiser.

"Oh my God, how many was that?" Sun asked.

"Nine?" Spin said, unsure.

"Too many! That's expensive and three would probably have been enough."

"I don't know, that's the kind of volley I saw the Cool Angel launch," Spin said, making sure that the missile doors started closing and that the computer was still calculating their wormhole jump.

"The Angel has light missile launchers, what you launched were ten times the size," Sun said with a chuckle. "The Cruiser is launching countermeasures; our missiles are accelerating."

"We'll be moving faster than that cruiser in twenty-eight seconds," Sharon reported. "We are out accelerating them by about six percent. Our jump system will be ready in thirty-five seconds."

Spin's defence readout flashed several times, indicating that particle beams were raking their aft shields. "We're down to forty-eight percent on the aft dorsal shield," she said.

"Sending reserve power, the field is recharged," Sun replied.

"Should we start shooting back?" Mirra asked.

"Wait until we see what happens with those missiles, the Cruiser is taking evasive action," Sun said.

Spin was surprised as she saw seven of their heavy rockets destroyed by the Cruiser's countermeasures, then a flash of white light on the nose of their ship indicated that the last two detonated against their shields. "Their forward shields are down," she said, surprised.

"Fire, aim for the bridge," Sun said.

Spin could hear the rumble of all three of their turrets firing high explosive shells at a rate of thousands a minute, and she couldn't help but imagine how much money she'd have to put out to replenish their ammunition, especially if she decided to replace the dumb fire shells with smart ammunition.

"We're almost in position, about to make the jump," Sharon said. "I can't believe I might never have to sleep with that creep again."

"What?" Sun asked, staring at her station.

"Oh, we're stealing Sharon," Spin replied as she watched the hull damage on the Light Cruiser appear on her screen, the nose of the ship was about to lose containment as hundreds of shells ripped into the hull. "Her master took liberties."

"Ah, welcome to the crew," Sun said.

Spin flinched as the space through the windows lit up with a series of quick flashes and their aft shields went down. One of their main thrusters flashed yellow.

"Impacts back here, everything is still functional, but they've got a bead on our thrusters," Nigel reported.

"Entering our wormhole," Sharon said. "They will be able to see which direction we've gone in for about three seconds."

"All stations, cease fire," Sun ordered.

The Governor leaned back with a sigh. "That's not as easy as it looks."

"It's a lot more fun than I thought," Mirra said.

Spin sat back in her captain's seat, realizing for the first time that she was leaning right over her command station. "We'll be in transit for ten minutes. We'll do a couple more jumps to cover our tracks then we'll set out for someplace for supplies along the way."

"To where?" Sun asked.

"British Alliance Territory. I want to know what a city without slaves looks like."

THANK you for purchasing and reading Cool Pursuit: Chaos Core Book 2. Your support is critical to the continuation of this and other series. If you'd like to know more, please visit: www.randolphlalonde.com